HOME GROUND

JANE CHAUDHURI

MINERVA PRESS
MONTREUX LONDON WASHINGTON

HOME GROUND
Copyright © Jane Chaudhuri 1995

ISBN 1 85863 633 7

First published 1995 by

MINERVA PRESS
1 Cromwell Place
London SW7 2JE

Printed in Great Britain by
Antony Rowe Ltd., Chippenham, Wiltshire

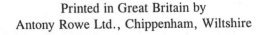

Home Ground

To my mother Patricia and my daughter Daisy.

Home Ground

Place - Wales

Time - circa 1870

THE MORGAN FAMILY

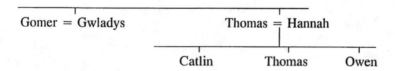

Gomer = Gwladys   Thomas = Hannah

Catlin   Thomas   Owen

THE REES FAMILY

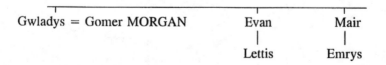

Gwladys = Gomer MORGAN   Evan   Mair

Lettis   Emrys

CHAPTER I

She straightened up with a small sigh, leaning back into the comforting restriction of her corset. The large, low-ceilinged room with its deeply-recessed windows seemed to lay itself out for her inspection. All was well arranged, well polished, well kept. The table, with its coarse lace tablecloth set generously for tea, gathered to itself a few scattered rays of the afternoon sun which was now bathing with brilliance the other side of the house. Her gaze came to rest on the mirror above the black slate mantelpiece. There she stood, Hannah Morgan, thirty-six years old and looking, if not younger than that, certainly not older. Her face was round, slightly flat and curiously immobile. The full mouth set firm, the dark eyes steady beneath strongly marked brows. In her high necked black dress with her dark hair arranged in a coronet of plaits she was a handsome woman, carrying with her an atmosphere of authority, of being in command of all around. She waited quietly and confidently for the arrival of her guests, one of whom, at least, she suspected of a wish to dispossess her. The sound of hooves, carried on the clear air, warned her of their approach.

The gig turned off the narrow road into the stony, well-marked lane which led down through the fields to the farm. Its four occupants were silent, each busy with their own thoughts. Beside the driver sat his wife. Her black bonnet framed a fair, plump face, which at first sight appeared good-natured until one noted the discontented droop of the mouth and the hardness of the pale blue eyes. Eyes which now looked with more than usual coldness at the substantial farmhouse set amidst its well kept pastures. Ty Garreg, the stone house, was a mixture of farmhouse and mansion. It had been built in the early years of the century by old Huw Morgan, the grandfather of the recently deceased owner. His grandfather had started married life in a *Ty unnos* - a one-roomed house built in a single night. House was perhaps too grand a title to give to what was essentially little more than a shack. Its thinly thatched roof resting precariously on four walls composed of a mixture of rough rubble and earth, muddied and strengthened with straw. But there was a small fire lit on a roughly fashioned hearthstone by the time the sun was up and the building itself was sufficiently stable to earn its builder squatter's rights, according to the ancient custom still prevailing at that time. Despite improvements carried out at more leisure, the house was never more than a one-roomed, clay-floored dwelling shared happily enough by parents, children and animals alike. But the site had been well-chosen, the family industrious and enterprising and by the time Huw inherited, he had lands enough and funds enough to take advantage of the boom years of the Napoleonic wars, when Welsh meat, corn, wool and timber found a ready market at higher prices than had ever been known before. Then Huw took all he had made and built the grand house he had dreamed of all his life.

The boom years soon came to an end and Huw's son and then his grandson could do no more than conserve what they had inherited, and were reckoned fortunate among their neighbours for being able to do so. Throughout the lean years Ty Garreg stood as a landmark among the other small farms and cottages and was still sufficiently imposing to reawaken a rage of resentful greed in Gwladys. Now she felt bitter resentment at the weakness of the man beside her. Gomer had been the oldest son and should have inherited Ty Garreg had he not stood aside for his younger brother. He had done this only to suit himself. Delicate and bookish, he had had no interest or liking for the hard outdoor life of the farm and had felt only relief when his younger brother showed his interest in these things.

After much perseverance, Gomer had achieved his ambition of becoming a solicitor and now practised in the market town which lay some four or so miles away from the farm. He was very happy there among his books and friends and usually Gwladys was content enough in the three-storey house in the narrow street which ran down to the quay. The house was both home and office and Gwladys relished the position that her husband's profession gave her among the town's minor gentry. But her brother-in-law's death a few months ago had reawakened in her an old dissatisfaction. She had never liked her sister-in-law, regarding her with suspicion as a foreigner about whom nothing was known. Now she saw her 'lording it' in what she considered to be her husband's, and therefore, her rightful home. Frantic attempts to make Gomer contest his brother's will giving the administration of the estate to Hannah had come to nothing and now she was embarking on more subtle ways to wrest at least some of the power from her sister-in-law's hands.

Behind her sat the two men whom she intended to use as allies. Her brother, Evan Rees, forty-five years old, with a narrow clever face and a high balding forehead had been a widower for three years. He had one daughter, approaching sixteen, who promised to be an adequate enough housekeeper but lately he had begun to mull over the advantages of marrying again. Lettis had been too young, and was now rapidly getting too old to take satisfactory charge of a house which often contained several young men. For Evan was a master tailor with many young apprentices. There was another factor to be considered. Evan had worked long and hard to make his business a success. He was now prosperous and had ambitions to rise in the world. The right sort of wife could help him acquire the sort of position in life he desired. He knew he would not be short of possible marriage partners, but there were few among his acquaintance who could match the advantages of Hannah Morgan. So he was more than willing to fall in with his sister's plans while determining that he and not Gwladys would be the main beneficiary of them.

Beside Evan sat his nephew, Emrys, a tall, rather stooping lad of nineteen. He had been apprenticed to Evan but on the recent death of his father he had come into a small inheritance, which had raised his horizons considerably. He was now hoping to enter his uncle Gomer's firm. Emrys was the second string to Gwladys's bow. For if Evan could not get the mother then, perhaps, Emrys could get the daughter. In either event her family stood to profit.

Only half aware of his wife's contrivances, Gomer contented himself with ignoring them. As they travelled down the drive to the house, his mind was full of painful memories of the sunny-natured young brother so suddenly lost to him. He had always felt grateful to Thomas for making it possible for him to escape the burden of a way of life that had held no appeal for him. His eyes lit up with wistful pleasure at the sight of two small fair-haired boys running to open the gate for their uncle. He and Gwladys had no children of their own and now he silently promised his dead brother that he would always treat his children as his own.

CHAPTER II

"Well then, sister, lovely to see you," gushed Gwladys, embracing Hannah with false fervour. Hannah stood stiffly looking past the embracer at the two men standing beside her brother-in-law. "Well now, sister," began Gwladys again rather nervously, "I was sure you would not mind me bringing my brother Evan and our nephew Emrys with us since they are just now staying with us while Gomer does some business for them."

"Not at all, sister," replied Hannah, nodding coolly towards Evan, whom she knew slightly, and towards Emrys, whom she knew not at all.

Once they were all seated round the table and the immediate enquiries about family and farm had been got out of the way, Gwladys decided it was time to bring her two protégés - neither of whom had yet said a word - more fully to the notice of her hostess.

"You may have heard, sister," she said, in a low confidential voice, "that despite my brother's sad loss, his business has grown and prospered exceedingly during the last few years. He is now considering expanding his premises and it is in connection with this that he has been consulting my husband. He is also considering, in the goodness of his heart, releasing our nephew from his apprenticeship and placing him in the way of becoming a solicitor. For Emrys now has a little capital of his own. My husband has offered to take the boy whether or not he can pay the fees; for as you know, sister, he is generous to his own default. But, alas, you cannot know how expensive everything is in the town, and Gomer and I are forced by his position to live in a certain style. So I have told him that he must get at least half fees, or the thing is impossible, and so it has been settled and Emrys will be coming to live with us from now on. I am, of course, only too eager to do what I can to help my poor sister in her bereavement. I brought the boy with me today to take his mind off the sad memory of his father's death. I also thought it would be a pleasure for Catlin to have someone young to talk to. She must get sadly lonely out here with no amusements or other young folk to help her pass the time."

Hannah's mouth visibly tightened at this little speech, but after drawing a quick breath she replied evenly,

"Catlin has her duties to keep her occupied and such amusements as are suitable to her age and station." Slightly alarmed at her sister-in-law's stiffness, Gwladys hastily agreed and asked where the dear girl was, for she longed to see her. At that moment Catlin came into the parlour shepherding her two little brothers who had been scrubbed into respectability. The boys gave only the most cursory greeting to the visitors while staring with very round eyes at the delights of the tea table. Catlin busied herself in preparing fresh tea. She was a slender girl of medium height, and like her mother was in unrelieved mourning; but where the dark clothes seemed to act merely as a background to Hannah's confident good looks, they served only to eclipse Catlin's more delicate beauty. Only her eyes still attracted attention. They were large, of a curiously light clear hazel and set in her small, pale face at a slightly slanted angle.

Emrys, who was not unaware of his aunt's intrigues, surveyed with interest this, up till then, unknown cousin. He had heard that the girl would bring a good marriage portion with her, for her mother was said to dote upon her. At first he thought her very gawky and plain but when, as she passed him a plate, he met the upturned gaze of those brilliant, slanting eyes, he felt a quickening of interest. He proceeded to set himself out to please and they soon discovered a mutual interest in music. Gwladys watched with satisfaction as the two young people drew slightly away from the group in order to examine the piles of sheet music which burdened the walnut piano. Hannah, watching her sister-in-law, wondered first at her expression and then understood. She studied the young man carefully as he listened attentively to Catlin's shy comments on some of the latest music she had received from Cardiff. She noted his slight stoop and tailor's pallor and thought impatiently, 'He will not do. If I give my Catlin away it will be to better than that. But why should I give her away? Why should she not stay here safely with me?' Then her eyes fell on her sons, still busily cramming their mouths with cake. When they came to inherit, what place would there be then for Catlin, except as an unpaid help to their wives and children. She had seen women leading such narrow lives too often for her to wish it for her daughter. No, the only safety for Catlin lay in a good marriage and to that she would help her; but she would look higher than a solicitor's clerk!

Looking away from the young people she met the considering gaze of Evan Rees. She recognised the approval in his gaze and this pleased her. In her turn, she considered him as frankly. Her steady gaze took in the aquiline face with its high forehead from which the hair was receding. Like his nephew he was tall and thin but, unlike Emrys, he did not stoop. Indeed, his shoulders were unexpectedly broad. For an idle moment Hannah let herself wonder what it would be like to relax against those broad shoulders to let them carry the burden of property which was her constant companion. With a little start, she recollected herself, 'Dear God, what was she thinking of? Was she to defeat Gwladys's matchmaking plans for her daughter only to fall victim to them for herself?' For she now saw quite clearly what her sister-in-law was about in bringing these two eligible men to her house. She could not yet see of what direct use it would be to Gwladys to see either herself or Catlin married, but benefit there must be or she would not have done it. So Hannah's manner to Evan was cool for the rest of his stay and she soon made the excuse of the boys' bedtime to send both them and Catlin from the room.

The room grew cool and its shadows deepened. Conversation faltered and Gomer, anxious to get home before night fell, suggested they should leave, to which the others, with varying degrees of reluctance, agreed. There was silence in the gig as it bowled smoothly along the high, narrow road. Gomer's mind, alone, dwelt sadly on the past. At the top of the hill he turned and looked back and down at Ty Garreg. Despite the young life it sheltered, it now seemed to him a lonely, haunted place. He knew it would be some time before he would have the emotional strength to go there again.

Evan Rees, looking straight ahead, saw not Gwladys's bonnet but the handsome figure of Hannah against the prosperous order of her home. So might his own home become could he only cultivate the interest which he sensed he had aroused in her. He began to consider carefully how best he might do this.

Young Emrys was thoughtful too as he calculated how much dowry the widow might be prepared to give to see her daughter married to a solicitor's clerk, who might very well have a prosperous future in front of him, assisted as he was by two such respectable uncles. He thought too, a little, of how insignificant Catlin had appeared until those brilliant eyes had met his. And he further reflected that money might not be the only pleasure or advantage that such a marriage could provide.

As for Gwladys, sitting so demurely in her stylish cloak and bonnet, she felt not entirely dissatisfied. A good start had been made. She now felt that she had allies in her campaign to bring Ty Garreg under her husband's control.

CHAPTER III

After the brief excitement of the visit, life at Ty Garreg quickly returned to its usual routine. Spring had come late that year and although it was nearly May there were lambs yet to be born and potatoes not yet planted. It rained for several days and Hannah stayed indoors, dividing her time more or less equally between kitchen and parlour.

Since she had come to live in the big house the grander rooms had been used as old Huw Morgan had intended, not shut up in dusty isolation as had happened in his successors' time when every year had seemed to bring harder work and fewer profits. Then Hannah had come. The mysterious bride from the far south with the inexplicably large dowry. She had flung open the doors and windows and with all the energy of her then eighteen years created within those square, shadowy rooms, a style of elegant comfort which had been the talk of the neighbourhood. The parlour, in particular was made a place of elegance and comfort. Here was Catlin's piano and her embroidery frame and Hannah would often sit beside her busy with some task of her own. But she could as often been found in the great kitchen where salted carcasses of beef and pork hung from the smoky rafters and barrels of salted fish stood in the corners. Here Hannah would work beside the two indoor maids, old Nest and young Non. Together these three could easily produce enough food for ten or forty, depending on the need. Daily the long wooden table would be laid with great bowls of potatoes creamy with buttermilk. Dishes of beef and bacon stewed with cabbage would be there also. Sometimes, to the delight of the boys, there would be dumplings, spiced with sugar and swimming in milk. It was well known that anyone who worked at Ty Garreg would eat as well and better than on any other farm around.

Since Thomas Morgan's untimely death the previous summer, Hannah had had to learn to order not only the kitchen and parlour but the farm as well. Old Ianto, the foreman, as gnarled as Nest was crabbed, had worked for Ty Garreg for almost as long as he could remember. He knew when and how to perform every task in the farm calendar. Yet he needed always to be reassured and directed. The reassurance and direction which he had once found in Thomas Morgan, he now found, to his surprise, in his widow. With Hannah's authoritative presence behind him he could find the necessary authority of his own to govern not only the regular farm workers but also the large gangs of itinerant workers which were needed from time to time.

While her mother was busy with her many tasks Catlin would sit at her needlework or play dreamily on her piano. A series of teachers and her mother's help had provided her with a reasonable education and it had been intended that she should tutor her two young brothers. But they had soon proved too unruly for her. So they had been sent to the little Church School which had been built on land donated by Thomas Morgan. There also, Catlin went on two afternoons a week. Not as a pupil, however, but as a Lady Visitor. She went ostensibly to help the big girls with their sewing but she spent at least as much time with the tiny children. The little ones that came from the low-roofed cottages that dotted the surrounding hillsides. With hardly a word of English between them they came into a world where they were forbidden to use the language in which their mothers spoke to them. Catlin's tender heart ached for their bewilderment, as it did for those poorer children who might have to tramp several miles to and from school with often only an onion sliced between two pieces of dry bread to sustain them through the long school day.

Next to the schoolhouse stood a four-roomed cottage. Here lived the schoolmaster with his widowed mother to housekeep for him. Mrs Roberts was a delicate woman, often ailing. Her husband had died young and her daughters married away. Her only son was now her sole support. Aeros Roberts was a stocky, black-haired man of twenty-eight with an agreeable puggish face. He had worked hard for many years to gain the qualifications that had made him eligible for the mastership of Maesbach School. It was, in actual fact, a position of almost unending drudgery. He taught, almost single-handed, upwards of seventy pupils ranging in age from four to fourteen years.

After school he had not only to deal with correction of the day's school work and preparation for the next, but he had to clean the schoolroom and carry coals, for there was no-one else to do it. Many of his evenings and weekends were monopolised by the Vicar, a tyrannical and lazy cleric who used him rather like an unpaid curate. For all this physical and mental drudgery, he received the tenancy of a small, inconvenient house, a meagre allowance of coal and a little less than two pounds a week. Yet Aeros, contrasting his present mode of life with past deprivations, had considered himself a successful man until one day he saw himself through Hannah's eyes.

Aeros loved Catlin. Had done so since the day he first saw her. His was a humble, wondering love. To him she was simply the most beautiful, most graceful, most angelic creature in the world. He had scarcely dared to dream that one day he might be more to her than her brother's schoolmaster. But his mother had not. With a mother's partiality, she considered her son good enough for anyone. She also loved Catlin and dreamed of a day when her son would have the wife he deserved and she herself would have another pair of younger, stronger hands to help her in those household tasks she found so tiring.

For a little while, mother and son continued happily in their shared yet unshared dream of a future centred around the young Catlin. One afternoon, Hannah, driving back from a visit to one of her tenant farms, decided to call in at the school and to collect her daughter, thus saving her the long walk back across the fields. As she drove up to the schoolhouse, Mrs Roberts ran out to greet her. The little woman's heart was pounding with excitement for she imagined that the widow had come to talk to her about their respective children. Rather surprised at her effusive greeting, Hannah asked where Catlin was. Trembling with pride Mrs Roberts led her distinguished visitor into the school room where Catlin and Aeros were bent in discussion over the register. Mrs Roberts looked at Hannah with shining eyes and said in a hoarse whisper,

"What a lovely couple they make!" Stiff with amazement, Hannah looked from Mrs Roberts to the young couple and back again. For a moment she could not believe what she saw in the woman's face. That she could dare to put her son on a level with Catlin and therefore, by association, herself on a level with Hannah!

She kept Catlin close beside her for the rest of the week, although she soon realised that the girl had no inkling of the Roberts' hopes. Her world was a narrow one and within it she had always been much doted upon. The affection and approval the Roberts had shown her seemed to her no more than was natural.

The next Sunday, after church, Hannah stood idly talking to the vicar outside the ancient church that had served the neighbourhood for more than seven hundred years. While seemingly engrossed in the Vicar's rather rambling conversation, she made certain that she stood where the Roberts would have to pass close by her as they left the church. As mother and son came by, Aeros with a shy greeting, his mother with a guilty blush - for she had quickly realised what an embarrassing error she had made in supposing that Hannah was in favour of a match between their two children - Hannah put out a gloved hand to stop them. Then speaking in clear, ringing tones which seemed to reach every corner of the old church yard, she said,

"Mr Roberts, the vicar, has been telling me how very small your salary is. Indeed, I cannot imagine how you live upon it. I would like you to know that you may call upon us whenever you are in need for I am glad to say there is always a surplus in Ty Garreg's kitchens!" Then turning her attention to Mrs Roberts she continued, "I have heard that you are very skilful with your needle and had thought to give you some fine work to complete that I have on hand, but then recollected that your hands, with all the hard work you have to do, must surely be too rough for handling such delicate stuff. But never fear, there is always plenty of plain sewing to be done for the house, servants' sheets and such like. Depend upon it, I will see you get your fair share." Beaming approvingly upon his charitable parishioner, the Vicar here interposed,

"Now then, Roberts, I hope you appreciate what a capital thing it is to live in a parish where one has such gracious and charitable neighbours to take an interest in one!" Unable to speak, choked as he was with anger and amazement, Aeros merely raised his hat and passed on. But Hannah was well satisfied. She had looked into his, eyes and had seen there a pride as stiff as her own. She knew that she could now, with perfect safety allow Catlin to resume her school visiting. There would be no proposals from Aeros Roberts.

CHAPTER IV

It was one of Catlin's school afternoons, therefore Hannah was alone when Evan Rees called at Ty Garreg. Hearing the sound of boots on gravel, Hannah looked up from her accounts to see his tall figure passing the parlour window. Hastily gathering up the papers, straightening her dress and smoothing her hair, she was amused to find her hands shaking. She grimaced at her flushed face in the mirror and mocked it gently - "To feel like this, my girl, after so many years and at the advent of a mere tailor!"

Then Evan was showed in by the little maid Non. Standing tall in the quiet room in his well-cut clothes, addressing her in his deep musical voice, Hannah realised that he was certainly more than a 'mere tailor'. For his part, Evan found Hannah as attractive as he had first thought, even more so, for now there was a vivacity about her, a lightheartedness of manner which he had not noticed on the previous occasion.

After a few words of conventional greeting, Evan explained his presence at Ty Garreg. He had completed his business and stay with Gomer at Newbridge and was on his way home. However, Gwladys had asked him if he could not make a detour of a few miles in order to call upon her sister-in-law.

Upon his agreeing she had entrusted him with various messages and gifts.

Among the packages were two dress lengths in the latest fashion for Hannah and Catlin. As the bright stuffs spilled out onto the tables Hannah felt a stab of anger.

"Mrs Morgan appears to have forgotten," she said icily, "that my husband has not yet been dead a year!"

Hastily Evan tried to retrieve the situation. "I am sure my sister did not intend any disrespect to your sad loss," he said. "But knowing that such quality is hard to come by in this part of the country, meant only that you should lay it by until such time as you felt able to take up again your rightful position in society!"

"That time may well never come!" replied Hannah sharply.

Evan could think of no more suitable reply than a sympathetic sigh. This was followed by an uneasy silence until he found the courage to murmur that, "Perhaps Miss Catlin might one day wish to return to wearing colours more suitable to her youth than the sad black she now wears."

"Indeed, Mistress Morgan," he continued as he regained his confidence, "it was about your daughter I particularly wished to speak to you."

Hannah raised her eyebrows in surprise. For a moment she thought 'Surely he cannot be a-courting Catlin at his age?'

Then Evan went on to explain, "I believe that you know my late wife and I had only one child. Since her mother's death

she has been cared for by two old servants. They are good,
faithful women, but I fear they cannot convey those refinements
of manner and pursuits that are suitable for a young lady.
When I met your charming daughter and observed her grace
and elegance, I realised only too well, how sadly lacking my
own poor girl is. Do not misunderstand me," he added hastily,
noting a certain wariness in Hannah's eyes. "There is no
unsuitable roughness about my daughter, only a childish
awkwardness which could soon be improved upon by genteel
companionship.

"I am about to make what is, I know, a bold request. Only,
let us bear in mind that we are, after all, related by marriage
and, indeed, might even be regarded as cousins. So do not
think it too outrageous of me, to ask if you and your daughter
could, at some time, pay us a short visit. Even a few days of
your company would be of benefit to my child!"

In some astonishment, Hannah informed him tersely that
since she was still in mourning she could not be expected to
make social calls.

"My dear lady!" cried Evan, "this is no social call, but an
act of charity to a poor, motherless girl. I pray you do not give
me your answer now but reflect upon it."

Hannah reflected. She now saw plainly enough that this
sudden interest in Catlin was merely a gambit to further his
acquaintance with herself. But perhaps after all, such a visit
might have its advantages. First of all, it would provide Catlin

with something else to think about than school visiting. Then, it would be pleasant to show off her daughter's accomplishments to a wider audience. It would also afford Hannah an excellent opportunity of finding out a good deal more about Evan Rees and his suitability as a suitor. So she did not definitely refuse the invitation but answered diplomatically, "You will realise, Mr. Rees," she said, "that I have many duties to fulfil in the management of Ty Garreg. But I will indeed further reflect upon your invitation and should I find it possible to delegate my responsibilities for a short while, then we may well make the visit." Evan saw that he must be content with this mild encouragement and soon after he took his leave.

CHAPTER V

By the next day Hannah had definitely decided against visiting Evan Rees. Indeed, she wondered how she could ever have considered it. Then came a letter from Evans repeating the invitation in the most formal and respectful terms. Enclosed in his letter was a rather blotchy and ill-spelt message from his daughter Lettis. In it, Lettis addressed Catlin as her 'dear cousin' and said how much she looked forward to her visit and hoped she would come soon.

Hannah still felt disinclined to accept the invitation but Catlin's excitement at the prospect of a town visit at last persuaded her mother to set in motion the complicated preparations that were necessary before she could absent herself from Ty Garreg. The little boys, she felt sure, would be happy and safe enough in the care of old Nest. The farm, however, was another matter. Ianto needed much counselling and much encouragement before he could face the prospect of being left in sole charge. However, at last all was settled and mother and daughter set off on the ten mile journey to Evan's home.

It was early afternoon when they reached Castell Coed. This was a pleasant little market town. Not so important or prestigious as Newbridge but it had a weekly market, one church, three chapels, two male voice choirs, a town band and a ladies' sewing circle. What delighted Catlin most, as she entered the town, was the High Street with its double row of bright little shops. She made a careful note of each one as they drove through it to Evan Rees' house which was nearly at the end.

Evan's house was tall and plain, with a flight of narrow stone steps leading up directly from the pavement to the double front doors. The rumble of iron clad wheels and the clatter of clogs on the cobbled road made the front rooms of the house noisy. Hannah was glad to find that she and Catlin had been given rooms at the back where it was much quieter. Here only a narrow strip of grass and a few stunted bushes separated the house from the river which flowed smoothly in its deep cut channel to where in the distance could be seen the hunched outline of an old mill.

Time, for the visitors, passed both swiftly and pleasantly. Lettis, from the moment she had noticed with awe the flounce of beribboned lace adorning the petticoat of her cousin, had fallen into a state of utter devotion. Catlin, who seldom had the companionship of a girl of her own age and social standing, found this admiration most pleasing.

Each morning, after breakfast, the girls would dress with great care and after admiring each other's toilette would set out to tour the High Street shops. Catlin had been well provided with pocket money, as had Lettis, and the two girls found the shopkeepers more than willing to let them spend hours browsing through their goods before making their small purchases. Once Catlin positively fell in love with a delicate, rose-pink parasol, but remembering in time the limitations of her mourning dress, bought it instead for Lettis. With tears in her eyes, Lettis promised that she would keep it for ever and ever.

When neither shopping nor visiting, for Lettis delighted in showing off Catlin to her small circle of friends, the two girls spent hours in earnest discussion of every aspect of their young lives. It was in Catlin's room with its dark old furniture and deep-silled window overlooking the strip of neglected garden, that one afternoon Lettis confided the deepest secret of her heart. Shaking her black curls forward to hide the blushes of her rather sharp featured little face, she spoke in whispers of her love for Emrys Hughes and his love for her. It took a little time before Catlin identified the handsome, noble youth Lettis described, with the pale, rather stooping young man who had visited Ty Garreg with her aunt Gwladys. Once she realised the two were the same, she felt a stir of uneasiness, remembering how Emrys had pressed her hand and gazed admiringly into her eyes as he said good-bye. She said nothing of this to Lettis but listened sympathetically as the younger girl spoke proudly of the promise Emrys had made to come back for her once he had become successful in his new profession.

This happy association between Lettis and Catlin left Hannah free to take full advantage of the excursions which Evan provided for her amusement. As she drove about the small town and surrounding countryside with him, she noted with approval the obvious respect in which he was held. His business interests had come to extend far beyond tailoring, although his expertise and knowledge of the trade was well known. But even outside his own spheres of work, his advice was sought on a variety of matters.

It was in this advisory capacity that they one day visited the old mill which Hannah had noticed from her bedroom window. She had then regarded it as no more than a picturesque addition to the scenery but now, as they came upon it at the end of a muddy little drive overhung with trees, she saw that it was decrepit, even decayed.

A red-haired, burly man, whom she took to be the miller, came out to greet them. After a few words of greeting, he eagerly drew Evan away to seek his opinion on some problem he was faced with. Hannah was left standing hesitantly on the threshold of the small, dark, crouched building. She wondered how anyone could live in such close proximity to the deafening crash of the falls which swirled furiously past its walls. She suddenly felt a touch on her arm, and catching her breath and looking down, saw a large, pale freckled hand splayed out on her black silk sleeve. Looking up, she encountered the mocking gaze of a young woman, broadly built and with the same red hair and pebbly grey eyes as the miller.

"Is it too noisy for you then, Mistress?" she shouted. "Come in, it will be quieter inside." So it was, but seated in the cramped, untidy room Hannah could still hear the gurgling, rushing waters that seemed to be trying to suck away the mill and the small spur of land on which it stood, in its rage to escape the confines of the countryside and make its escape to the sea.

The young woman said nothing more, only stood with folded arms surveying her with an insolent, sardonic gaze which Hannah found intolerable. She was about to get to her feet and go outside again when Evan reappeared with the girl's father. Their business was concluded and, after a few civilities, they were once more out in the clear, sunny air, away from the damp, overhanging trees and the rushing waters.

As they drove away Hannah asked Evan about the miller and his daughter.

"Oh, they are good enough people!" he answered carelessly. "They have not been here long. They come from some place on the coast. Quite a long way from here. Forty miles or more. I've heard they are a strange lot there. *'Y plant Y lle'* - the children of the place, they are called by folk round about, who say that, from isolation and interbreeding, they have all come to look the same - red-haired and bold mannered. You probably noticed that in the girl. I understand she has already got herself a rather dubious reputation around here. However, that is no business of mine. As for the father, I have found him an honest enough fellow and, in his small way, a good business man."

When Sunday came, Evan asked his guests whether they wished to attend the English church or would they accompany him to chapel. On her marriage to a professional man Gwladys had changed her Sabbath habits but her brother still kept with the chapel in which he had been reared and was, in fact, one of its most active and influential members. Without hesitation Hannah told him she would prefer to go with him to chapel. She saw this as another opportunity to learn more about Evan and his way of life.

As they walked through the iron gates and across the square of neat grass to the plain yet handsome building, Hannah was pleasantly conscious that she and Catlin were the cynosure of many feminine eyes as well as masculine ones. As she took her seat she was complacently aware that her dress and bonnet were the most stylish and probably the most expensive in the congregation. Yet, she noted with approval, that there were others that nearly approached their standard. Indeed the worshippers, she observed, were overwhelmingly respectable and many obviously well-to-do. She told herself that it would be easy to become accustomed to this place of worship. Her own opinion in this matter was all that concerned her, for although Hannah accepted as unquestioned fact the existence of God and was even prepared to accept that it was her social as well as religious duty to make regular attendance at a place of worship, the manner in which she carried out that duty she believed to be entirely her own affair.

On the last afternoon of their stay Evan asked Hannah to drive out with him. This had been a daily occurrence throughout their stay but Evan's request seemed a little more urgent and his manner just a little nervous. Hannah realised that this drive was important to him and dressed with even more than her usual care.

As they reached the end of the long straggling high street, Evan turned the gig sharply left into a narrow lane that led upwards by rapid twists and turns. At the top of the hill they left the lane and went through a gate that led onto a wide, grassy plateau. Here Evan helped Hannah down and invited her to admire the view. It was well worth admiring. For there, not far below, laid out in a tumble of roofs and chimneys was the whole of the little town, bordered by its winding river and cradled in the encircling hills.

"Here," said Evan, "is where I shall build a new house. I have engaged a skilled architect from Cardiff to draw up the plans. By next summer it should be ready for occupation. It will mean for me, not only a new home but the start of a new style of life. Will you not share that life with me?"

Turning her head away, Hannah looked out over the town. "Ty Garreg," she said softly, "is a good house and already built. It is surely a good enough place for any gentleman."

"That it well may be," cried Evan urgently, "but it is too deep in the country for me. I must be of the town if not in it. Times are changing, Hannah. Wales is changing, stirring, waking from her sleep. We have been neglected, ignored for too long. Out of all these feelings a new Wales will be born. Then there will be opportunities and important places to be filled by men like me. The old gentry have distanced themselves too far from their Welsh roots. New times call for new leaders. Men who can argue in both Welsh and English. Men who are successful in their lives yet have not forgotten the traditions in which they were reared. I am such a man, Hannah, and with you beside me I could go on to great things. Tell me, how would you like to spend part of each year in London? Meeting and entertaining great and famous people? Becoming one of them? Think not only of yourself but of the opportunities for Catlin."

Hannah thought and saw in her mind's eye Catlin, most beautifully dressed and surrounded by eligible and elegant young men. She was impressed by Evan's speech and began to feel an answering stir of excitement. But she only said, "I have too many responsibilities to consider change lightly. It would all require much management. Also, as I am still in the first year of mourning, it would be as improper for me to receive your advances as for you to make them!"

"Then I will not do so!" smiled Evan, not displeased with what he felt was a favourable reaction to his proposal. "I ask only that you reflect on what I have said and at some not too future time indicate that we may return to this subject."

CHAPTER VI

Back again at Ty Garreg, Hannah did indeed reflect upon Evan's words. Reluctant as she was to leave the lovely place, she saw clearly enough the advantages of accepting his proposal. She was not, she had to admit, head over heels in love with him. But she liked him, even found him attractive. She believed in his confidence in himself and knew she could help him achieve his ambitions. Above all, marriage would give her a more assured place in a wider society than she knew at present. Catlin would have a much better chance of making a good match than she had now living at Ty Garreg.

There were, however, many practical difficulties to be overcome before she could think of remarriage. Entailed as it was upon her sons, she could not sell the farm. It would be easy enough to find a tenant. The Welsh were notoriously eager, often unwisely, to take on more land. But on the whole, she would prefer to put it in the hands of a farm manager. In that way, she could still exert control even though at a distance.

So gradually and almost unconsciously, she accustomed herself to the idea of leaving Ty Garreg and becoming the wife of Evan Rees. Yet still she felt much hesitancy in the matter. When messengers came from him with parcels of delicacies from the town and letters of increasing affection, she acknowledged them with only coolly civil notes.

The summer, which had been so long in coming, suddenly blazed into glory. The hay in the great meadow was cut and stacked in seemingly unending sunshine. Even Ianto had to admit that it was all most quickly and easily done.

It was a busy time for Hannah as she helped the women provide enormous meals for the hay cutters. It was with some relief that, on the last day, she left the maids to clear up the kitchen and walked out into the peace of the late afternoon.

There was no wind, the air was warm and the sweet scent of freshly mown hay was everywhere. As Hannah walked slowly round the house she noted how well the great corner stones fitted into one another. Running her fingertips over the grooves she remembered the poet's description of the house of Owain Gln Dwr.

Conjointly are the angles bound
No flaw in all the place is found.

'No flaws indeed,' she thought, 'except, that it is not entirely mine and can never be Catlin's.'

She walked further down to where the fruit bushes were already displaying tiny berries. As she bent to examine them a shadow fell across her. Turning and straightening she found herself facing a stranger. Her startled gaze took in a mass of red gold hair, clear grey eyes, a red scarf knotted around a strong throat, a spread of shoulders; but all these sightings were taken in separately like pieces in a kaleidoscope which would have to be steadied before they made a whole. It was as if she had met with some species of being she had not known existed.

The young man (for that was all it was) stared back at her with interest. With her hair tucked back under a kerchief and her black work blouse unbuttoned at the neck, he took her for one of the house servants. Apologising for startling her he asked where he might find the master of the place.

While he spoke Hannah regained her composure. She saw now that he was after all only a man, if an uncommonly handsome one. About 24 or 25, a working man, yet not quite a peasant. His accent was strange. It reminded her of someone, some place - she could not quite recall. She asked him what he wanted. He answered frankly and cheerfully, that he was in need of food and shelter and added that he was willing to work for it.

Hannah felt a strange disinclination to declare her identity. She turned and walked silently back through the kitchen garden. Her black skirt caught now and then on the thorns of fruit bushes, disturbing and releasing the fragrance of the leaves, flowers and herbs that grew alongside the path. The man walked behind her, also not speaking but apparently quite at ease, as his bright gaze swept critically and appreciatively over the many signs of prosperity and careful husbandry. When they reached the end of the path she told him to go round to the kitchen at the back of the house and that she would arrange for him to be seen.

It was some time before Hannah was satisfied that she presented a sufficiently respectable and imposing appearance to deal with this unexpected caller. At last, dressed in her best black silk, she went down to the parlour where she rang the rarely used servant's bell to summon Non. When the little maid appeared, rather more rosy cheeked than usual, Hannah told her to send the stranger in.

While seated at the kitchen table, flirting with Non and teasing Nest, the stranger had already learnt that Ty Garreg had no master but only a widowed mistress. He was not, therefore, surprised on entering the parlour to find an elegantly dressed woman sitting there. What did surprise him was to recognise her as the woman he had met in the garden. He wondered why she had said nothing to him then as to whether she could give him work or not.

Hannah addressed him in distant, business-like, tones. He answered all her questions in the same frank, easy manner he had used in the garden. He was, he told her, part sailor, part fisherman. He had also had farmworking experience, for his grandmother had owned a small hill farm and had often needed his assistance. After she died the farm had been sold so the proceeds could be divided among her seven daughters, "…and precious little of that came to my Mam!" he added wryly. So now, when trade at sea was slack, he had to search elsewhere for a place. This time, larger numbers than usual of Irish itinerant workers had come over for the season and he had had to travel farther than he had ever done before in search of work.

A few more questions satisfied Hannah that he did indeed have a fair knowledge of farmwork. When they had finished speaking, she sat for a while staring silently down at her desk. Then abruptly she made a decision. Raising her head she met his clear, untroubled gaze.

"You may stay here on a week's trial. During that time you will make yourself useful to my foreman. It will depend upon his opinion as to whether you stay here any longer. There is a loft over the barn where you may sleep. I will see that it is supplied with a pallet and blankets."

Well satisfied with this arrangement and congratulating himself on having fallen on his feet, the young man cheerfully made his way to the kitchen where he proceeded to wheedle from Nest as large a plate of food as she was able to produce.

At the end of the trial week Ianto had grudgingly to admit that he could find no actual fault with the new hand's work. Indeed, Alun Ifans proved himself to be an intelligent and willing worker. He possessed the happy characteristic of being able to make himself agreeable to everyone. Young Non sighed romantically for him. Old Nest pitied him for a motherless lad. He made Ianto feel a very fount of knowledge and practical skills; as indeed he was. Even Trefor, the rather loutish cowman, fell under his spell. As the two men worked together, the sailor would talk to him in a comradely fashion, sharing with him the varied experiences of his roving life. Something of his breezy confidence would brush off on the stolid countryman. He would walk home across the fields to his poor cottage filled with too many children, and there would be something like a swagger added to his usual plodding gait. And as for Hannah - she looked into her parlour mirror and said to her sad reflection, 'Don't be a fool, girl. I thought I told you, never again.'

Then she took up her pen and wrote,

> *'Dear Evan Rees,*
>
> *It would give the children and I great pleasure to see you once again at Ty Garreg...'*

CHAPTER VII

During the next few weeks, while Hannah waited for Evan's reply, she kept much to the 'gentry' side of the house. Old Nest grumbled that she had never known Mistress take so much looking after. For nowadays, Hannah seldom ate at the long kitchen table but had herself and Catlin served in the parlour. Catlin too, was kept much occupied by Hannah. All day long the girl ran here and there, delivering messages and fetching and carrying as Hannah took up one occupation after another. Yet despite all she so willingly did, Hannah continuously found fault with her.

One hot and sultry day with thunder rolling in the distant hills, Catlin seeing Hannah, as she thought, immersed in her accounts, asked timidly if she might not go down to Ysgol Maesbach. She had hardly been there since they returned from Castell Coed and soon the school would be closing for the holidays. Some of the big girls she helped with needlework would be leaving and she wished to see that they left school with at least one piece of completed work. This modest request provoked a violent outburst from Hannah which so upset and terrified Catlin that she ran crying from the room.

Hannah, as shattered by the outburst as her daughter had been, sat staring at the shadows deepening around her. At last she stirred and sighed, 'How unreal everything seemed. What had she been doing to let things get to this pass!' She tidied her hair at the mirror and then went upstairs to make her peace with Catlin.

When she reached the girl's door she paused and listened to the muffled sobbing. She reached out her hand to turn the knob, hesitated then turned and went along the corridor to her own room. There she took a worn leather case from a drawer and sat deliberating for a while over its contents. There were not many to consider. At last she selected an old garnet ring which Thomas Morgan had given her when she first came to Ty Garreg. He had placed great value on it for it had been in his family for three generations. She could no longer wear it for her fingers were not so slender as they had been. She folded the ring carefully in a clean linen handkerchief and placed it in her pocket. Then she went along the corridor to make her peace with Catlin.

Making peace with Catlin was, as always, an easy matter, for the girl could not bear to be on bad terms with anyone, least of all her mother. The present of the ring delighted her, for she knew its history.

"Oh mother," she said, "I shall wear it always in memory of my father. I am sure he would like that!"

"I, too, am sure he would, my girl," said Hannah, resting her cheek on the soft brown hair.

The next day a letter arrived from Evan Rees apologising for the delay in answering her own. He had been away when her letter arrived at his home. He promised to come and see them as soon as his business affairs allowed.

Hannah, who had begun to fear that Evan had grown indifferent to her, was both relieved and delighted. With his letter tucked into her bodice she felt armoured against the clouds of misgivings and uncertainties that had threatened to overwhelm her. Once more she moved confidently between field, kitchen and parlour, supervising and ruling in all the interlocking spheres of life at Ty Garreg.

The potatoes and other root crops had been, she decided, neglected. A gang, of women and children were set to hoe between the rows. There were arrangements to be made for the harvesting of the winter wheat which, despite its late start, promised to be a good one. She now discovered how much, in her absence, Ianto had come to depend upon his young assistant. Where once he would have sought her opinion, he now often turned to Alun Ifans. At first this annoyed Hannah but she soon realised that the young man's opinions were worth having and so she too gave them due consideration.

Nowadays, when she looked at the sailor she saw only an ordinary young man.

Good-looking perhaps, but too young. 'Why do I say too young?' she thought, 'what is his age to do with me? And ill-educated.' His English uncertain and his Welsh tinged with that curiously rough tone that she now remembered belonged also to the people at the mill she had visited with Evan Rees.

The days passed pleasantly and busily. Hannah even found time to take more notice of her little sons. She realised, with some disquiet, that they were growing up with speech and manners that did not accord with what she considered to be their station in life. She thought of the old grammar school in Newbridge and resolved that they should be sent there as soon as her own affairs were settled. In the meantime, she set them daily tasks in reading and composition, greatly to their disgust for they much preferred to run wild in the freedom of the fields and barns.

For his part, Alun Ifans was grateful for any distraction that took Hannah's attention away from the work of the farm. For privately he considered it a monstrous inversion of the rightful order of things that a woman should be set above men. He allowed that Hannah was a fine looking woman and a clever one, but it would be more seemly if she would stick to house and kitchen and not attempt to order men about. He thought nostalgically of red-haired Modlen whose interests had never strayed from those he considered suitable for a woman. And thinking, of her (whom he had thought little enough of when he was with her) he was suddenly shaken with a painful longing for his own salt aired place and his own people. So unlike these dark-haired country folk. He vowed that as soon as he had enough money he would be back there. Where he could be his own master and perhaps set up home with Modlen; or someone as near like her as made no difference.

CHAPTER VIII

The sun shone brightly the day that Evan's gig bowled smartly down the road to Ty Garreg. Beside Evan sat Lettis, sheltering beneath the precious pink parasol. As she saw Catlin come out to stand beside Hannah on the front steps, she waved the parasol in enthusiastic greeting, but Catlin hardly noticed it for her eyes were fixed on what followed the gig. Held on a leading rein was a gleaming chestnut pony, her silvery mane and tail tossing in the light wind.

As Hannah noticed the rapt expression on her daughter's face she felt a sharp stab of guilt, remembering how she had promised to buy Catlin a horse to replace the fat pony, long outgrown. With so much else to occupy her mind the promise had been forgotten by her but not by Catlin. During those long talks in the lazy afternoons at Castell Coed she had told Lettis how her father had said he would take her to the annual horse fair so that she might choose a new horse for herself. But before the fair came round he had suffered that insignificant gash on his hand which had so swiftly provided a gateway for the virulent germ that had caused his agonised death less than two weeks later.

Her mother had afterwards promised that she herself would see that Catlin had a new horse. Time, however, had passed;

no new riding pony appeared and it seemed to Catlin that her mother had either forgotten or regretted her promise.

Now here was Evan, smiling so kindly down at her as he placed the leading rein in her hands. Catlin looked at her mother. Was it possible, was it right for her to take this lovely gift? Hannah's smiling eyes told her it was so. Hardly staying to say 'thank you' Catlin called Lettis, and the two girls and the delicately stepping little mare sped off to the cool green paddock that already housed old roly-poly Punch.

Their departure left Hannah and Evan standing alone together in a sudden quiet. For a moment, Hannah felt a curious shyness and hesitation, then seeing Ianto crossing the yard, called sharply to him to come and see to the gig. This small exercise of authority restored her composure and she turned to Evan with a coolly gracious smile and invited him to enter the house.

That first slight awkwardness passed, the day went well. The dinner was a simple masterpiece; lamb fragrant with herbs, a pie dish tightly packed with cherries under a crisp golden crust. Evan pushed his chair back from the table in a state of well-being such as he had not known for a long time.

As he looked around, all was pleasing to his eye. Hannah, a picture of comely dignity in her gleaming, black silk. Catlin, her hazel eyes wide with excitement lighting up her small face with a beauty he had not noticed before. There would be little trouble in finding a good match for such a girl, he thought.

Even the little boys, their fair heads bent together as they counted cherry stones, awakened in him feelings of sentiment. A man need feel no shame in introducing such sturdy handsome lads as his sons. And although it was a pity that the farm was not entirely in Hannah's hands, the entail did mean that he would not have the burden of assuring the boys' futures. In the meantime, the income would provide a welcome addition to his own. He felt he must congratulate himself on making such a wise choice. Now his dearest wish was to get the whole matter settled.

While the boys played in the grassy meadow and the two girls worshipped at the shrine of 'Gracie' as Catlin had christened her new pony, Hannah and Evan sat together in the parlour and talked long and earnestly. The sun slipped away behind the house and the room grew shadowy. No formal proposal had yet been made, nor any formal acceptance given, yet somehow it had come about that all was settled.

Hannah was discussing, with keen enjoyment, the furnishing of the new house, a possible school for the boys, new occupations for Catlin, when Evan, although also enjoying discussing these things, felt obliged to recall her to present practicalities. The paramount problem, an he saw it, was the lack of a farm manager for Ty Garreg. He chided Hannah gently for not having, so far, made any serious attempt to find one.

"It is not an easy matter," she protested, "to find a man both competent and trustworthy, and content to give his all to Ty Garreg and yet never aspire to own it himself."

These words encouraged Evan to put forward his own solution to the problem.

"I was lately at my sister's house in Newbridge," he told her. "She said to me how very much she would like to live in such a house as Ty Garreg. Her husband's business has prospered and now takes up too much of the house for their comfort. He has an efficient head clerk and, therefore, does not need to be at Newbridge all the time. Gwladys says that he would do anything in his power to safeguard the interests of his little nephews. Indeed, he wishes constantly that they were his own. Can you not see, that here offers an excellent solution to our problem? Gomer would never wish to take over Ty Garreg and rob his nephews. It is true that he is not a farmer, but he was born in this place and must know the workings of it."

Hannah listened to this speech in silence, sitting quite still, her face expressionless. Inwardly she was consumed with a rage so violent that she felt in danger of collapse. She had been well aware for many years that Gwladys envied her the status of Ty Garreg. She recalled the unkind reception the older woman had given the young, nervous girl whom Thomas Morgan had so unexpectedly brought home as his wife. The rapid Welsh conversations carried on over her head, while she was still stumbling through what was to her a little used language. She remembered the sneering remarks made on the too early time of Catlin's birth. She also remembered, with what she took to be a flash of brilliant insight, the satisfaction on her sister-in-law's face as she had watched Evan and her in conversation. Had not that first meeting been brought about by Gwladys? And was she now to get her reward for her complicity?

Now her rage could no longer be contained. It burst out in a flood of invective breaking over the astonished head of Evan Rees. Her unwillingness to give up Ty Garreg, her bitterness at the terms of her husband's will, her resentment against her parents' too ready bestowal of her on Thomas Morgan and their continued ostracism of her; all these feelings which had seemed half-resolved, half-forgotten, now rose up in her stronger than ever. All this lent force to her fury and point to the accusations of complicity with Gwladys which she hurled at Evan.

The unhappy object of her attack sat white-lipped, staring in disbelief at the transformation of the stately, well-bred comely lady of Ty Garreg into this ranting virago. He watched with distaste and a little fear, the dribble of spittle on her lips, the clawed hands, the bared teeth. At last he found the courage to rise to his feet and search desperately for his hat and bag. But Hannah preceded his departure. Rushing down the hall, she sent the great front door crashing back on its hinges and called wildly for Ianto to harness the gig.

Within a few minutes the yard was full of activity. A shocked Ianto attempted with trembling hands to harness Evan's high-spirited mare in the gig. The two girls had run to the spot on hearing Hannah's screams. Now Lettis stood clutching her pink parasol, tears raining down her face. Catlin, although she had in the past experienced something of her mother's temper, had never witnessed such a scene as this, and could not think what to do. As Evan walked, still shocked and shaken, towards the gig, Hannah watched him from the open door. Quite suddenly her anger had left her; driven forth by her total exhaustion. She leant against the door post for support and what happened next passed before her eyes in seeming slow motion with the inevitability of a dream.

The little boys suddenly burst into the yard, shrieking with excitement as they pursued a rabbit which they had succeeded in hunting out of the long grass. The terrified little animal, seeking refuge, rushed beneath the feet of the mare which had already been made nervous by Ianto's rough handling. Now thoroughly alarmed by the boy's shrill voices and the presence of the small animal beneath her feet, she neighed wildly and reared in the shafts just as Evan was placing his foot on the step. Caught off balance, he fell beneath the wheels and flailing hooves. The mare would have bolted, rolling the gig completely over him had not Alun, running from the side gate, caught the trailing rains and pulled her up. As soon as she was standing quietly, he bent and dragged Evan from beneath the wheels.

As he knelt upon the ground supporting Evan's head, Hannah, still anaesthetised by her exhaustion, stood watching. She felt no shock, no anxiety, only a wild pleasure as she noted how the muscles rippled under the tanned skin as the sailor lifted the unconscious man. And as she watched him being carried towards her she could only wonder how she could ever have thought of Evan Rees as being strong and sheltering.

CHAPTER IX

An anxious few days followed as Evan lay unconscious in the vast curtained bed which had belonged to Thomas Morgan's parents. Slowly his senses returned to him and it gradually became clear that beside the many cuts and bruises on his head and face, the only injury of any account was a badly sprained ankle.

At first as Evan lay in a half-bemused state, he had no recollection of the violent scenes which had preceded his accident. Then, as slowly the memory of Hannah's distraught state came back to him, he found it difficult to reconcile the images his mind presented to him with the quiet caring woman who stayed almost constantly by his bedside. Her very appearance contradicted her past behaviour. For, without giving any explanation to anyone, Hannah had abruptly discarded her deep mourning and although not yet in full colour, the soft greys and pretty lilacs she now wore softened her features and went well with her sweet, quiet manner. It seemed to Evan impossible that such a woman could ever have snarled like a wild cat, spat at him, screamed abuse.

In his semi-invalid state, Evan had plenty of time to think. He now saw clearly enough how his sister had been manipulating him for her own ends (as she had often done in their childhood). Indeed he had half-realised this before, but since her schemings had fitted in well enough with his own inclinations, he had not pursued his suspicions. Now the realisation that there had been at least some partial truth in Hannah's accusations made it that much easier for him to excuse her and to accept her evident desire to put all bad feelings behind them.

Catlin had been surprised by her mother's sudden abandonment of the mourning which she had previously been so insistent upon. But she was glad enough to follow her example. Dressed again in light and pretty dresses, the girl looked very different from the pale and sorrowing waif who had haunted Ty Garreg for the past year. Her very steps seemed lighter as she sped about the place, always with Lettis in close attendance.

One fine morning, wandering in the kitchen garden, she noticed how full and red the raspberries were. She picked some, cradling them in green leaves in a small basket, and decided to take them to Mrs Roberts whom she had not seen for some time.

Hannah raised no objection to her taking Lettis with her to visit the Roberts and as the girls set out in bright sunshine they were in a happy holiday mood. They made a pretty picture as they crossed the fields in their summer dresses, Lettis twirling her parasol and annoying Catlin by trying to steal berries from the basket. When they reached the schoolhouse, Catlin leant upon the low fence which surrounded the small garden and laughed aloud to see the sober school master in shirtsleeves and with tousled hair, digging up his potatoes. At first, Aeros was a little put out to be so discovered but as he looked at Catlin his heart was so moved that he forgot his own appearance completely.

He had loved the grave girl in her sombre black but Catlin, in sprigged muslin with blue ribbons in her straw bonnet, was more beautiful than he could ever have imagined. During the past year the heavy mourning had disguised how much the girl had grown and changed. The last traces of childhood had vanished; it was a young woman who now leant laughing on the fence. The slenderness of her beribboned waist, the curve of her cheek, the indentation left by the wicker basket upon the soft arm, were all entrancing to him.

When they went in to meet Mrs Roberts, she was more reserved. Catlin in her grown-up clothes had, if not a resemblance to Hannah, a fleeting shadow-like impression of her which reminded the older woman of her humiliation in the churchyard. So although she was, as always, kind and pleasant towards the girl, she paid more attention to Lettis and before the afternoon was out was dreaming dreams that involved Lettis and Aeros and wedding suits cut by the bride's own father.

As for Lettis, she had no such illusions. Her sharp black eyes had soon perceived that Aeros was hopelessly in love with Catlin. On the way home she teased her cousin with her discovery. Catlin was at first incredulous, then doubting, and finally pleased and flattered at having an admirer. From then on, she thought a good deal about Aeros Roberts and in her thoughts he grew more handsome and more impressive than in reality he was.

Unaware of her daughter's romantic dreaming, Hannah continued her efforts to regain the confidence and regard of Evan Rees. For once again she saw him as a safe refuge from dangers she only half admitted to herself. She set out her accounts for his perusal and sought his advice regarding her small investments.

Flattered by her obvious respect for his business acumen, Evan was in his turn impressed by her intelligent grasp of monetary matters. He again realised how well she would manage his own domestic matters. His first wife had been a simple girl. Pretty and amiable, but inclined to carelessness and extravagance. Throughout his married life, Evan had felt it necessary to deal with the financial management of his household as well as those of his business. With Hannah as his wife he would be able to leave the domestic finances in hands as capable as his own.

Once again he grew eager to bring forward the marriage day. The greatest immediate difficulty was the future management of Ty Garreg. In his heart he considered the suggestion made by Gwladys to be the most practical but he was not so foolhardy as to mention that proposal again to Hannah. So he set about finding another solution.

During his convalescence, Evan had often felt the need of a strong arm to lean on as he moved slowly about the house and garden. Alun Ifans had often been called on to supply this. Evan was already grateful to him for saving him from possibly more serious injury and Alun's cheerful and helpful assistance increased his regard for him. Like Trefor, he soon fell under the easy charm of the sailor's personality. He noted with approval how quickly the young man mastered any new task that was presented to him. He also discovered that he was literate to a greater degree than most of his class.

One evening, as Evan and Hannah sat in easy companionship watching the last rays of the sun on the distant hills, he asked her if she had ever thought of appointing Alun Ifans as farm manager. Completely surprised at this suggestion Hannah bent her head over her embroidery to hide her sudden confusion. Then in a voice made deliberately casual, she said she did not think the young man was suitable for such a heavy responsibility.

"But indeed he is," insisted Evan. "I have watched him most carefully. He is honest, industrious and very quick to learn. He is well liked by the other servants and I am sure he is most devoted to your welfare."

"Why on earth should he be so?" queried Hannah, "I hardly know him."

"Indeed, I think you do not," said Evan warmly. "I pride myself on having some knowledge of human nature and I tell you, this young man is fit for much greater responsibilities than he has at present. I strongly advise that you consider my suggestion most carefully. For otherwise, I do not know how this marriage of ours is to come about."

Hannah considered and the longer she did so, the more attractive and feasible the plan became. To a man like Alun, without capital or influential friends, the position of farm manager at Ty Garreg would indeed be a glittering opportunity. His inexperience would necessarily demand some guidance but that could be given by herself and Ianto. Here she felt a kind of fearful pleasure as she imagined herself and Alun engaged in long discussions over the affairs of Ty Garreg. So it was settled between herself and Evan that she should engage Alun Ifans as a trainee farm manager. A few days later, now limping only slightly, Evan drove away from the farm well-pleased with how matters were progressing.

CHAPTER X

After Evan and Lettis had gone, the house seemed strangely empty. Hannah, preoccupied with planning the future management of Ty Garreg, left Catlin much to her own devices. The girl, missing the constant companionship of Lettis, attempted to take up again the tutorship of her little brothers. But she had neglected this duty too long. Owen and Thomas had developed new interests and they far from welcomed her efforts to teach them. When she attempted to settle them at some craft or lesson they would often defy her and take the first opportunity they had to escape into the fields to roam and play with their schoolfellows from Maesbach. When Catlin sought her mother's help to enforce her authority, Hannah told her not to worry about it. They would soon be going to a new school where, hopefully, the schoolmasters would beat them into shape.

Catlin, feeling unwanted and lonely, spent a great deal of her time with her new pony. Day after day she practised riding through the green fields which encircled the house until she felt confident of riding further afield. At last, she felt she could ride as far as the seashore.

Riding up the hill which sheltered the house from the sea winds, she turned right on reaching the top. The lane ran

steeply downhill for about a mile, then skirting the yard of a
tenant farmer, plunged even more steeply, becoming narrower
as it did so until it was no more than a stony track. At last,
leaving the fields, it passed through a grove of rowan trees,
their berries glowing a fiery orange in the sunlight, and their
low branches brushing against horse and rider.

Now bushes and trees growing high on either side met
overhead, making a shadowy green tunnel. Only the smell of
ozone betrayed the nearness of the sea. In the heavy shade,
flies buzzed and pestered, so both girl and pony were glad
when the vegetation ended abruptly and they found themselves
standing on the sloping, rocky incline which led down to the
sandy bay enclosed by towering cliffs. The place was seldom
visited so Catlin was surprised to see a man sitting alone on a
rock staring out to sea. She hesitated and considered turning
and riding back up the lane but the man, alerted by the clatter
of hooves, jumped up and turned round - and then she saw it
was Alun Ifans.

With his usual cheerful helpfulness, Alun ran up to take the
pony's bridle and help it negotiate the rocky incline. Once
safely on the sand he helped Catlin dismount and dusted a rock
for her to sit on. He seemed to take it for granted that they
would sit and talk together.

At first the two young people's conversation was stilted and
general, until Alun admitted that he often tried to spare an hour
from his work in order to visit the seashore. Surprised by this

admission Catlin asked him why he liked the lonely place so much. Most people she knew, avoided the sea, finding it at worst menacing and at best bleak.

"Bleak!" exclaimed Alun, "Far from it. It is both rich and promising. I tell you I can hardly bear to live without the sound of it in my ears, the smell of it in my nostrils and taste of it in my mouth."

Then he told her how much he longed for his home village and described it to her as well as he could. He pictured for her a straggle of cottages clinging to either side of a narrow valley cut deep into the cliffs. Along the bottom of the narrow valley flowed a crystal clear stream which finally lost itself in a shallow pebbly bed on the beach. At the very end of the village, perched on a grassy ledge which overlooked sea and beach, stood the cottage where he had been born and lived with his parents and three sisters.

"We lived well," he boasted, "for my father was not a poor man. My grandfather had left him ten ounces in the finest fishing smack in the village, and my mother's family owned land."

"What on earth do you mean by talking of a ship in ounces?" asked Catlin.

Then Alun explained to her the system whereby the value of the large and expensive fishing smacks, thirty or forty tons in size, were divided into sixty-four shares or ounces. These 'ounces' were as valuable as land and like land often remained in the same family for generations. They were rarely sold unless there were no direct heirs. Often they would be used as marriage portions.

Alun's father's legacy was regarded as a large one, for each of the ten ounces he inherited represented four shares in a good-sized fishing boat. His family were able to live well until the day the boat went down in a sudden squall taking his father and elder brother with it. The family was now dependent upon the grandmother and what she could spare from the proceeds of her small farm. Alun, at eleven years old, had to help out as much as he could by working at whatever small jobs he could get.

Until he was sixteen, he divided his time between working as a farm labourer and helping the local fishermen. Then he got a job as a deck hand on a small coastal steamer. At first he would come home at the end of each voyage and give his mother all the money he had happened to save, which was often nearly all his wages.

One by one, his sisters left home, going either into service or marriage. Gradually the voyages he took grew longer, the visits home more infrequent, the savings smaller. The last visit had been at the end of a particularly difficult voyage which had taken two years. He came home to an abandoned cottage with only two simple crosses in the churchyard to greet him. Mother and grandmother had died within six months of each other.

Filled with grief and remorse, he determined to turn his back on the sea. He was unpopular in the village because of what people saw as his neglect of his widowed mother. There seemed nothing to keep him there any longer so he set off inland.

After some months of wandering, picking up casual work where he could, he had arrived at Ty Garreg. Since he had been living there he had felt calmer and happier but of late he had begun to dream again of becoming a man of property, a 'holder of ounces' as his father had been. He knew that one day he must return again to his home village and live as his father had done.

"But how that is to be brought about," he laughed, "on the wages and savings of a farm labourer, is beyond me!"

"Oh, but you will, I am sure of it!" cried Catlin, who was much moved by his story. "I have heard mother speaking with Mr Rees and I know they have plans for your advancement. But I think, perhaps," said Catlin doubtfully, "you should not tell her of your wish to return to the sea."

And so the young people found much to talk about as they walked backwards and forwards across the small landlocked beach. Catlin's heart swelled with sympathy and admiration as Alun told her more of his history and ambitions. She admired the red gold of his hair and thought that his eyes were the silvery grey of the sea under a cloudy sunset. And he, looking at the softness of her flushed cheeks and her hair, loosened and tangled as it was by the rowan trees, wondered why he had hardly noticed her before.

That first encounter was followed by many others. Catlin rode down to the shore almost every afternoon. She would often find Alun there and they would wander together among the rocks searching for small sea creatures or walk from one end of the beach to the other, laughing at the contrast between their footprints; his so broad and large, hers so small and narrow. And as they walked along the sands or rested an the rocks, Alun would describe to the awe-struck girl the many foreign places and peoples he had seen. As she compared his many experiences with her own uneventful life, Catlin asked,

"How can you stay in this quiet place when you could be somewhere half-way across the world?"

"Oh, it's grand to have seen these sights and to know about them," he told her, "but there's a contentment, a happiness that can only be found in your own place, among your own people. I want the sea for a neighbour now, not a master." It became more difficult, however, for Alun to slip away from his work to meet Catlin by the shore. Hannah was making increasing demands upon his time. At first, he wondered why she troubled to discuss farm matters so often with him, and why she insisted on him accompanying her to the weekly markets. Then one day, calling him into the parlour, she bade him sit down as she had a proposition to put to him.

Then she told him that she was considering making him farm manager at Ty Garreg when she married Evan Rees in the spring. He would live in the house and his salary would be, if not overwhelmingly generous - for Hannah managed to retain her good business head - at least much higher than it was at present.

Hannah watched as her handsome servant's face became suddenly shuttered, withdrawn, his grey eyes wide and blank. As he stared past her at the window she imagined he was gazing at the green fields of Ty Garreg but instead he was seeing in his mind's eye - a blue sea and a pebbly shore and himself at the wheel of a sturdy craft, steering her home. The impossible dream had come quite unexpectedly, almost into reach.

As Alun returned slowly to the everyday world, he felt a rush of gratitude towards Evan Rees. He suspected that he had had much to do with influencing Hannah's decision. He also became conscious of Hannah's voice asking rather sharply for his comments on her proposition. Then indeed his thanks came tumbling out in a torrent of excited words. Hannah felt a warm glow of pleasure at being able to please him so much, at giving him so much happiness. A pleasure, however, which was marred by the realisation that he so obviously felt no regrets at the thought of her coming marriage and resultant removal from Ty Garreg.

As Alun came out of the shadowy house into the sunshine of the yard, the thought came to him that Catlin would now be at the beach; if he ran down to meet her he would be able to tell her about his wonderful news. But, even as he laid his hand upon the gate, a warning chill struck him. Despite Hannah's encouraging words he had sensed some other emotion, a reluctance perhaps, regarding this new employment of his. Perhaps she still regarded him as little better than a farm labourer. Should she suspect him of over-familiarity with her cherished daughter, she might well change her mind regarding his suitability as a farm manager.

'No,' he thought, turning away from the gate and crossing to the barn. 'It would be better not to meet Catlin on the shore today, or for many days to come.' So on that golden afternoon, Catlin waited on the beach feeling suddenly alone and forlorn. Hannah bowed her head upon her desk and wept as she realised that all she had done was to make Alun eager for her departure in order that he might come into his good fortune. And Alun, he sat on his pallet bed in the dusty barn and worked out, in the back of his Sailor's Bible, how many years he must work at Ty Garreg before he could truly go home.

CHAPTER XI

Alun's avoidance of Catlin was made easier for him by an invitation she received from Lettis, who was planning a very grand party to celebrate her sixteenth birthday and wrote that she could not think of doing so without the presence of her 'dearest friend'. Mildly puzzled by her daughter's reluctance to accept the invitation, Hannah decided to ignore it and within a few days, Catlin was on her way to Castell Coed with instructions to buy herself and Lettis the prettiest gowns that small town could provide.

As Hannah turned away from waving farewell to Catlin, she felt an almost exhilarating sense of freedom. Her little boys, for the time being, hardly entered her consciousness. Indeed she hardly saw them these days, dividing, as they did, their time between kitchen and fields. And now she was to be free of Catlin's observing presence.

To Alun's surprise, for he had expected to continue sleeping in the barn until Hannah's departure from Ty Garreg, a room was made ready for him in the house. Nor did he any longer eat at the long table with the other servants, for Hannah said that she had such frequent business to discuss with him that it would save time if he ate with her in the parlour.

Partly resentful, partly scandalised at Hannah's intimacy with a farm worker who had, after all, only recently come among them, the other servants now treated him with surly suspicion. Although they did not dare to openly disobey his orders, they carried them out in a sullen and uncooperative manner. Alun, naturally gregarious and sweet tempered, was unhappy at the isolation thus forced upon him. He also began to view Hannah with suspicion. She had bought new clothes for him. Good quality, sober clothing, suitable, she said, for a farm manager of an important estate. As yet, however, there had been no more money, no increase in wages. As he sat, uncomfortable in his new stiff clothes, facing Hannah across the polished table, Alun wondered what she was trying to make of him. What did she want of him?

Alun was not a conceited young man but even he was at last obliged to admit to himself that the dominant reason for his promotion had to be the fact that Hannah was attracted to him. And that she was in every way, excepting only the direct words, offering herself to him.

Alun, as always, took his problem down to the seashore and there sat on a rock, furrowing his brow as he attempted to analyse the implications of this unlooked for situation.

He considered Hannah herself. She was older than him, but still a most attractive woman. Had she been of his own class, he would have had little hesitation in accepting the opportunity of a brief affair with her. But she was not of his class. She was a lady and above all she was his employer. If he became her lover, would she not be simply using him as gentlemen sometimes used their female servants? Could his pride accept this? But perhaps he was mistaken. It could be that she was more serious, that she meant marriage. That would make him master of Ty Garreg.

Master of Ty Garreg. Truly a dazzling prospect. Money and land. But would it really be to his benefit? After all, he had no wish to remain at the farm any longer than was necessary. During the last few months his obsession to recover the status his father had lost had grown enormously. Would Hannah help him regain it? He thought not. Her passion for the land was as strong as his was for the sea. But then, if they were married, he would be master. It would be for him, as head of the household to decide where, and in what fashion, their lives would be spent. If he decided to go back to the village, then it would be Hannah's place to go with him.

At the thought, his good humour returned and he laughed aloud at the picture presented to him of the elegant Hannah living in a fishing village. Keeping house for a fisherman, wearing a shawl like the other wives. What would folk make of her? What would they think of him? No. There was no way that was possible. If they married they would have to stay at Ty Garreg.

But what would their lives be like there? What would be the reactions of their neighbours both rich and poor? Where would his place be? With the gentry or the working folk?

Then he began to consider the effect on those most closely involved. He thought of Evan Rees. During the time of Evan's stay at the farm he had grown to like and respect the quiet, reserved man who, in recommending him to his present position, had obviously trusted him. Surely, he would consider that he had betrayed that trust. There were the little boys. Now they liked him well enough but when they grew older their attitudes might change. And above all there was Catlin. How could he face her if she came home to learn that he would soon become her stepfather. Stepfather! He laughed again, but there was a sourness, a bitterness in the laugh.

Alun felt a sudden, almost overwhelming impulse to seek Hannah out. To tell her frankly, face to face, that he wished for no closer relationship between them than that of employer and manager. But what if he did this thereby spurning her, as yet unspoken, offer? Would she continue to employ him, in any capacity let alone that of manager. He would be out in the world again, penniless and without work or reference.

He buried his head in his hands and groaned aloud. To hell with women! Why could they not keep to the simple role in life for which nature had intended them? He resolved that in future he would have as little to do with Hannah as possible. He would keep out of her way and hope that marriage to Evan

Rees or some other fortunate happening would prevent either Hannah or him from committing any serious acts of folly.

Alas for these wise resolutions. Within the week they had been forgotten. He was a young man and alone and when one night Hannah called him to her room, ostensibly to hunt down a mouse, he went willingly enough.

It was not long before the women servants noticed how seldom his bed was slept in. Now all their scandalised suspicions were confirmed. The resentment, which had previously centred upon him as being the stranger amongst them, now switched to Hannah. They began to remember that Hannah, having come among them a mere twenty years ago, was little better than a stranger herself. The house became a place of sidelong glances and malicious whisperings. Only Ianto refused to join in their spiteful gossiping. He kept himself apart, still trying to believe in the good faith of the mistress who had always treated him with kindness and understanding and in the young man whom he had come to look upon almost as the son he had never had.

CHAPTER XII

On her arrival at Castell Coed, Catlin's low spirits soon revived. For no-one could have failed to be pleased with the ecstatic welcome Lettis gave her, or the quiet but equally genuine welcome she received from Evan Rees.

To further distract her from her melancholy she was soon swept into the hectic preparations Lettis was making for her birthday party. She had persuaded her father to let her invite every young person of any consequence for miles around. She was determined to make it the most splendid function of its kind that had ever taken place in that area.

Scolding, and in her turn being scolded by the two elderly servants, she swept through the house like a small tornado, insisting upon perfection in every detail. At last, with every corner swept free of dust, with every conceivable surface polished, she turned her attention to the question of refreshments. There was much hunting down and borrowing of recipes, the making and remaking of lists, and the discussion of menus. Then the two girls, armed with their much amended lists, sallied out one morning into the High Street to visit those shops they deemed worthy of their patronage, and very pleased indeed were the owners of those shops to receive their custom. Without exception they all promised delivery at the earliest possible moment, opened doors, bowed to their young customers and then stood rubbing their hands with satisfaction at the prospect of shifting those 'luxury' items that had hung about their shelves for so long,

The house shone like the proverbial new pin. Dishes were either resting on marble shelves in the capacious larder or preparation for them was well under way. Now came the most important moment of all, the final fitting of their party dresses. Miss Petty, the town's premier dressmaker, had been pinning and tucking for days and was herself well pleased with the results. Lettis, in dotted Swiss, embellished with rose-pink ribbons, was a pretty sight. Catlin was beautiful. In one of the little shops she had discovered a length of silk in a rare shade of *eau-de-nil*. The colour complemented her pale skin and turned her eyes sea-green. Even Lettis's loyal little heart could not escape a pang of envy when she saw the other girl in her lovely dress.

As if the party itself was not excitement enough for Lettis, a letter arrived which sent her into a very ecstasy of happiness. Emrys Hughes wrote to say that he would be coming to visit her on her birthday as he had some business to discuss with her father.

"He is coming to speak for me. I know it. I know it!" and Lettis whirled round and round, apron strings and black curls flying as she danced for sheer happiness.

Witnessing her friend's exhilaration, Catlin felt an almost irresistible impulse to tell Lettis about her own relationship with Alun Ifans, to let her know that she was not the only girl young men sought after. But even as she opened her mouth, doubts assailed her. What, after all, was her relationship with Alun? What were his feelings towards her? He had spoken much to her about his future but had never once hinted that she would have any place in it. Perhaps she had only imagined a tenderness in his eyes when he looked at her, a lingering in his touch when he helped her across the rocks. She would only be shamed if she let Lettis know that she admired a young man who did not think of her. So Catlin wisely held her tongue concerning her own possible romance and soon forgot her brief impulse to compete with Lettis.

Came at last the morning of the great day and Emrys Hughes with it. His consciousness of the superiority of his new occupation had increased his self-confidence. Somehow he seemed to stand straighter. Good food, for Gwladys for all her faults, kept a good table, and new clothes further improved his appearance. Catlin, remembering the pale youth who had visited Ty Garreg, was rather impressed by this new-style Emrys. He was both pleased and startled to find Catlin staying with Lettis. He had by no means forgotten her but remembering the formidable Hannah had lacked the courage either to write or call upon her. He now found himself in a quandary. Here he was with Catlin in such an approachable situation yet, at the same time being so obviously claimed by Lettis as her suitor.

Emrys had indeed come to Castell Coed with some half-formulated plans concerning Lettis. He liked her and found her open adoration of him endearing. He regarded her father as an up-and-coming man; as he also believed himself to be. It would be a most suitable match. Now here was Catlin upsetting things by being so much more attractive than he remembered her and making Lettis in comparison look no more than a pretty child. He decided to say nothing of his feelings to either girl for the moment, and to treat Lettis as coolly as she would allow!

Evening came to Castell Coed and through the summer dusk the young guests began to arrive. The sons and daughters of farmers came in from the surrounding hills on horseback or in pony carts. The town guests - the doctor's son, the minister's daughters, the children of respectable shopkeepers - walked sedately in their party pumps along the narrow pavements to where the double doors stood wide open at the top of the flight of stone steps leading into the tall grey house. Through that doorway came a blaze of light, the sound of laughing voices and above all the sound of music. The party pumps quickened their steps in their eagerness to be among the revellers, to be part of that favoured group which had been invited to celebrate the birthday of Miss Lettis Rees.

For a while Lettis was so busy receiving and unwrapping presents, exchanging news with those she seldom met and gossip with those she met almost every day, that she hardly noticed the absence of Emrys from her side. Then, as the last stragglers arrived and the young people began to drift into opposing groups, girls on one side, boys on the other, Lettis saw the opportunity, so much looked forward to, of presenting her almost fiancé to her admiring and probably envious girl-friends. But where was Emrys?

Hurriedly, she searched for him. She must find him before the dancing dispersed her audience. He was not in the parlour or in the breakfast room. He was not in the hall or seated on the stairs. At last she found him in the kitchen watching admiringly as Catlin, with deft fingers, prepared yet more platefuls of party delicacies. As she called him to her side only a sharp note in her voice betrayed her annoyance at what she saw as a social backwardness in Emrys; for as yet she did not suspect him of any attachment to Catlin.

However, as the evening wore on, Lettis found her sweetheart often too far from her side and too near to Catlin's. There was a lull in the dancing and Lettis suddenly realised that she was alone once more. Across the room she could see Emrys solicitously handing a glass of fruit punch to Catlin.

She stared suspiciously at her friend, noting for the first time how different she looked from everyone around her. Against all those bright and blooming girls in their beribboned dresses,

Catlin was as pale and lovely as a white rose. Her ash brown hair hung down unringleted. Around her slender neck she wore a string of ivory beads which in the soft lamplight merged into the pale green of her silk dress. The only note of strong colour came from the garnet ring which as always, she wore upon her right hand.

Lettis who had been so confident, so sure, so triumphant even in her belief that all was going to be perfect for ever and ever in her own little world, felt her heart contract with misgiving as she gazed on the pale beauty of this suddenly strange Catlin.

As if she had received a summoning message, Catlin suddenly lifted her head and stared across the room at her. Alarmed at the girl's pale and stricken expression, she came quickly to her. She took her friends hands in hers and told her she was the luckiest girl in the whole world to have such a wonderful party, and the cleverest girl in the whole world to have so well arranged it. And Lettis was comforted, reassured and almost perfectly happy again.

CHAPTER XIII

It was agreed by everyone, that the birthday party had been a great success. For a good while after it was the talk of Castell Coed and the surrounding area. It became a sort of landmark in time. People referring to this or that happening would say that it took place at a point in time either before, or after the birthday party of Lettis Rees.

Lettis was quite aware of the stir she had caused. She was satisfied that her debut into young ladyhood had been so well celebrated that no-one in the neighbourhood could avoid being conscious of it. Everyone, and especially the young men, must now be aware that she was of marriageable age and was, moreover, a 'very good catch indeed'. Not, of course, that she wanted to attract other suitors for did she not have already a very satisfactory one in the person of Emrys Hughes?

At the thought, however, a small doubt crept into her mind. Was he so very satisfactory? For it must be admitted that Emrys had changed. No longer did he press her foot under the dinner table or squeeze her waist when no-one was looking. Since his arrival he had said nothing of their great plan for the future. In fact, he seemed to want to avoid the subject when she referred to it. He did not, however, avoid her. Far from it. Wherever she and Catlin went, however trivial the errand or tedious the occasion, he was their willing escort.

Moreover, he made no move to return to Newbridge. Long after all the other guests who had been invited to stay in the house for the party had left, Emrys was still there. He could have been said to have 'outstayed his welcome', at least as far as Evan Rees, who was of a thrifty nature and saw no sense in entertaining guests beyond their normally expected length of stay, was concerned.

But despite some chilliness in his host's manner as they met yet again at the breakfast table and some rather pointed advice regarding homeward travel, Emrys remained firmly implanted in the Rees household. Surely it could only be, thought Lettis, that he was simply waiting for the right moment in which to approach her father and request her hand.

One day Emrys himself suggested an excursion. He asked Lettis if she had shown Catlin the place where the river, which wound so smoothly and placidly past the house, became a raging torrent as the deep-cut river bed turned itself into a series of rocky steps. When she heard that salmon could be seen there leaping the falls, sometimes as high as ten feet, Catlin was eager to visit there. Lettis, wanting as always to please Emrys, agreed and they set out immediately after lunch. The weather was hot and overcast and long before they reached the falls they were all tired and thirsty. A state which the sight of the foaming river did nothing to alleviate. In fact, it made it worse as they imagined the sparkling waters pouring down their poor dusty throats. Emrys gallantly volunteered to go and see if he could persuade a friendly cottager to provide them with tea and the girls sank down thankfully upon the grass to await his return.

He returned, rather later than they had expected but flushed with triumph. He had found the cottage wives neither as friendly or as obliging as he had hoped and had been about to give up the search for tea when he had met a young woman coming out of the short drive which led into the mill. To his relief she had agreed to provide them with a meal and was even now preparing it. He did not add that the price, settled upon in advance for these refreshments was, in his opinion, extortionate. Their weariness forgotten, the girls leapt to their feet and hastened to tidy their hair and dust down their dresses as best they could.

It was a merry little party that crossed the old bridge and walked through a dense clump of trees to where the crouched, shabby building stood on its rocky platform above the turbulent waters. As they entered the dark little room where they were to eat, Catlin felt none of the oppressive atmosphere which had so disturbed Hannah on her visit earlier in the year. To let in more light and air, Emrys pushed open a small, thick glassed window which looked out over the river.

The air which came in was fresh and cold and brought with it a shower of fine spray which spattered the dresses of the two girls. Raising her voice so as to be heard above the roar of the waters, Catlin cried excitedly that it was 'just like being at sea'. Not that she had ever been at sea but her long conversations with Alun Ifans had made her feel that she almost had.

The food, when it arrived, was better than Emrys had gloomily feared. Cold salmon, good bread and fresh butter washed down with quantities of strong tea, pleased all their healthy young appetites. For the first time the trio seemed to be in one accord and their bright, happy voices competing with the noise of the falls, lit up the dark old room.

A glance at the pocket watch, left him by his father, reminded Emrys that they should leave shortly if they were to be sure of arriving home before dark. After some whispered conversation with the red haired young woman who had served them, the two girls withdrew into another room. When they returned they found her alone clearing the dishes. She greeted them familiarly saying,

"Your sweetheart has gone outside." Then looking full at them with her bold grey eyes, she laughed and added, "though whose sweetheart he is might be a mystery to some, even to you young misses, for he seems to court you both the same!"

"That is not so!" blurted out Lettis impulsively.

"Is it not indeed?" sneered the woman. "Is it you that he courts then?"

"Yes, it is. Though it is nothing to do with you!" answered Lettis, angry with herself for having been drawn into so personal a conversation with a stranger and a social inferior at that.

"Well, you're wrong there, Miss," said the woman spitefully. "It's the brown haired maid he fancies. You can believe me, for I have a knowledge of such things. Which is more than you two have, that's easy to see!"

Much put out by this exchange of words, the two girls hurried outside to where Emrys was waiting with some anxiety as he saw how rapidly the shadows were deepening. He had no wish to become more unpopular with Evan than he already was. And he had a suspicion his host would not take kindly to his daughter and her friend wandering the lanes after dark.

On their way home he wondered what had happened to their merry party. Neither girl spoke much and Lettis was particularly sharp in her manner towards both him and Catlin. He could only conclude that the long walk had over-tired them and resolved that he would lead them on shorter expeditions in future.

That evening Catlin went to Lettis's room and sat on the bottom of her bed as she used to do when she first visited. As she did so, she realised how seldom she had done this lately. She felt a little stab of fear. Suppose she and Lettis were never to be friends again? How would this affect their future lives together? How could she then live in this house? But she would have to because her mother was going to marry Evan Rees. There was no other place for her to go. She must make

Lettis believe that what the mill girl had said was nonsense. Make her love her and want her for a sister again.

So Catlin set out with all the charm she was capable of to make Lettis believe these things. She was successful to the point that the two girls went downstairs with their arms round each other's waist and at least on the surface Lettis appeared to be as loving a friend as ever.

During the next few days, however, further cracks appeared in the facade of their friendship as Emrys became somewhat bolder in his approaches to Catlin and more neglectful of Lettis. Any slight pleasure she may have previously taken in his conversation or company was now as nothing to Catlin against her fear of a serious quarrel with Lettis and the implications this held for their future together. She wrote to Hannah imploring her to send for her. She said she was homesick, that her duties at home were being neglected, that her pony must be missing her.

Hannah had no wish for Catlin to return at this juncture of her relationship with Alun and wrote back coldly rejecting all Catlin's reasons. "She was not," wrote Hannah, "to reject the many kindnesses the Rees family were showing her, simply because of a mere childish whim. She must at least stay out the month for which she had been invited." Despite her misgivings, Catlin could do nothing but accept her mother's ruling.

One evening, after the lamps had been lit, the two girls sat at the table amicably discussing new trimmings for their bonnets.

Emrys moved restlessly about the room, picking up and examining one object after another. He looked at the girls who appeared, at the moment, to be completely oblivious as to his presence. As if making a sudden decision, he left the room and went in the direction of Evan's study. Lettis, who had not been as indifferent to his presence as she had appeared, stopped comparing the little bundles of flowers and ribbons and clutched at Catlin's hand.

"He has gone to see father," she whispered. "Can it be - it must be about me!" Hoping most fervently that it was, Catlin did her best to soothe her friend's impatience but with little success. However, Lettis had to contain her curiosity for the rest of the evening. When Emrys and Evan finally joined them, the former looked downcast and the latter grave and preoccupied and spoke of nothing but the usual gossip of the day.

The next morning at breakfast Emrys was very subdued in his manner. To the girls' surprise he told them that he would be leaving that morning.

"My uncle needs my assistance and has asked me to return with all speed!" he announced importantly. Both girls knew that he had received no communications from Newbridge and could only assume that his sudden departure had something to do with his interview with Evan on the previous evening.

Emrys was soon packed and away leaving Lettis in tears and Catlin feeling very uneasy indeed. Closing the door firmly after his one-time apprentice, Evan looked grimly at the miserable spectacle the two girls presented. Sternly he told Lettis to go to her room and make herself presentable and Catlin to go to his study. Seated before his desk, Catlin studied Evan's narrow, rather severe face, and asked herself whatever he could have to say to her. Evan stared back at her with a certain irritated impatience that he should find himself involved in this matter when he had so much more important business to attend to.

Abruptly he told Catlin that Emrys, knowing that Evan was soon to become her stepfather, had asked him for her hand in marriage. Seeing Catlin's look of complete astonishment, for she had not guessed that things had gone this far, he asked her if Emrys had not mentioned the matter to her.

"Never, never!" answered Catlin vehemently.

"Well, at least he has shown some discretion there!" observed Evan. "Now tell me, do you have any fondness for this young man?"

"No, no, not at all," stressed Catlin, and then glancing hesitantly at Evan asked, "what did you say to him?"

"I told him," replied Evan, "that I had, as yet, no authority over you and that if he wished to pursue his suit, he must approach your mother. But..." and here for the first time a hint of amusement softened the stern lines of his mouth, "for some reason he appears to be more in awe of that lady than he is of his old master. So it may well be a little time before you are honoured with a visit. I further advised him, that in view of the circumstances, it would be better if he returned to his duties at Newbridge."

Now, totally abandoning his severe air, he continued, "My dear girl, I do not want to displease either you or your mother. I hope you will feel that I have dealt with this matter correctly."

"Oh, indeed I do," breathed Catlin. "I have no wish to be married for a long time yet, and least of all to Emrys Hughes!"

"Well, then all is settled and there is no need for us to discuss it further. Put it out of your mind and think only of enjoying the rest of your stay with us," said Evan kindly. Then seeing Catlin's suddenly stricken face, he asked impatiently, "What is it now, girl?"

"It is Lettis," gasped Catlin. "I do not know what I shall say to her. But, of course, you do not know - I should not have said anything!"

"Of course I know," snapped Evan, "I am not so blind, or deaf, nor so old as that young lady seems to imagine. But he is not the first young man she has wasted her time dreaming over and I dare say he will not be the last. Take no notice of her tantrums, she will soon be over them."

But Lettis had to be taken notice of. She was most bitterly hurt by her suitor's defection. She felt she hated him, but she hated Catlin even more. All her suppressed jealousy of the older girl now came to the surface and resulted in a series of vitriolic attacks on her. There was no reasoning with her and at last Catlin abandoned all her attempts at reconciliation and ran to Evan Rees and begged him tearfully to send her home to her mother. So obviously unhappy was she that Evan felt he could do no other than arrange this. Cursing Lettis for her hysterical behaviour and Emrys for his meddling, he bade Catlin an affectionate farewell, promising to call on them as soon as his commitments allowed.

CHAPTER XIV

On the long drive home Catlin had plenty of time to reflect upon the recent events as they affected her. Nervously, she wondered if her mother would blame her for what had happened. She wondered whether, in fact, she had been at all to blame. Had she unwittingly encouraged Emrys in his mistaken affections? She did not think so, but Lettis did and perhaps others, even her mother, might agree with her.

As they drew nearer to Ty Garreg, Catlin noticed how much the countryside had changed in the few weeks she had been away. The sun shone but with a more mellow light. Grass and flowers had a faded, tired look about them. Roses, past their best, trailed their thorny branches through tall, wiry grass and dusty bushes. Already the leaves were changing colour and beginning to fall from the trees. Here and there, little drifts of them lay upon the road and made a whispering sound beneath the wheels. Until now, Autumn had been to Catlin a barely noticed interlude between the pleasures of summer and the excitement of the Christmas season. Autumn meant the provision of new warm clothes, of a house suddenly full of flickering shadows as the fires were lit. The discussions between her and her mother of what crafts they should choose to keep them pleasantly occupied in the warm house during the harsher months ahead. Now for the first time she was aware of the poignancy of the season that foreshadows the close of a year that will never come again.

She did not, however, have too long to indulge in these melancholy thoughts for across the fields came running Thomas and Owen, home from school. They were delighted to see Catlin and their exuberant welcome immediately revived her spirits. As she hugged their sturdy little bodies, she wondered how she could have missed them so little and silently congratulated herself that from time to time during her shopping expeditions she had seen some small things that she knew would please them and had, most happily, bought them. How awful if she had left this present buying to the last and had had to come home empty-handed. Then with a small boy on either side she ran into the house. The boys shouting, "Catlin is home, Catlin is home!"

Hannah was coming down the stairs as they ran into the hall. For a moment she stood quite still and stared in shock at Catlin and in that moment, Catlin, looking at her mother's face, thought 'she did not want me home.' But then Hannah ran down the last few stairs and put her arms round her and held her tightly saying,

"I am so glad you are here. I have missed you so much. You must never go away again!"

Nervously, Catlin explained why she had had to come home and to her relief Hannah did not seem to blame her or, indeed, to take the episode at all seriously. When Catlin told her that Evan Rees would be coming to see her shortly, she retired to her parlour and wrote him a brief note begging him not to neglect his business affairs to worry about this childish squabbling. She was sure that their daughters would soon be the best of friends again.

"However," she added, "it might perhaps be better if the girls were kept apart for a little while to allow time for tempers to cool." She hurriedly sealed the letter and gave it to Evan's groom to take back with him.

Suddenly released from care, Catlin ran happily about the place. First to the kitchen, where rather to her surprise - Nest embraced her tearfully. Then to the paddock where, perhaps influenced by the apples she carried for her, the pony gave her a gratifyingly warm welcome. On the way back to the house she met Ianto and Trefor who both appeared glad to see her. She would have liked to ask them the whereabouts of Alun but a curious shyness prevented her from doing so. She consoled herself with the thought that they were bound to meet at the long table at dinner time.

As the time for the evening meal approached she changed her dress and tidied her hair with more than usual care before going down to the kitchen. The air was full of fragrant steam and there was all the usual hustle and bustle which preceded a meal going on.

"What shall I do to help?" she asked Nest.

"Are you eating with us then?" the old woman asked.

"Why should I not?" answered Catlin in surprise.

"How am I to know? It's parlour folk in the parlour and kitchen folk in the kitchen, and some who are neither one thing or the other these days," grumbled Nest.

"What do you mean? What does she mean, Owen?" appealed Catlin to her brother who had just emerged from under the table - a favourite hiding place with him.

"She means are you going to be kitchen folk like Thomas and me, or are you going to eat in the parlour like mother and Alun?" explained Owen.

"Like Alun?" repeated Catlin in amazement, "Why should Alun eat in the parlour?"

"You may well ask, girl," snorted Nest, banging an iron pot down on the long scrubbed table, "And maybe I could answer you if such things were fit for young ears!" But here Ianto, who had been sitting quietly in the high-backed settle, leapt up and told her,

"Hold your tongue! And you, girl," he added, "go to your mother!" Which Catlin in some bewilderment did.

She found Hannah in her bedroom, brushing out her long dark hair.

"Mother, Nest wants to know whether I am to eat in the kitchen or in the parlour." Hannah did not answer for a moment but putting down her brush, started, with deft fingers, to coil her long hair into its usual coronet of plaits.

"Where do you think you should eat, Catlin? With the servants or with your mother?"

"I want to be with you, of course, mother, but we nearly always used to eat all together," replied Catlin. "And why does Alun Ifans eat in the parlour now?"

Watching her reflection in the mirror as she carefully placed the last few hair pins, Hannah spoke evenly, "Alun Ifans is being trained for the post of farm manager. I think it better that he now keeps himself at a distance from the other servants. This will serve to give him more authority in their eyes."

"But father never felt he had to keep himself separate from his men to have their respect!" said Catlin, feeling oddly disturbed at the new mode of life that appeared to have come about while she had been absent from Ty Garreg.

"That was entirely different. Your father did not have to establish his superiority, it was already evident. Although," added Hannah thoughtfully, "it did often occur to me that it would have been more seemly if he had not been quite so intimate with the servants. It was not so in my old home, I assure you!"

Catlin opened her mouth to reply to this, to her extraordinary statement, but was quickly silenced by Hannah. "That is quite enough. I will have no arguments on this subject. Obviously, you will have to dine here with us. Go and tell Nest so!"

Hannah and Catlin were already seated when Alun came in. Taken completely by surprise, Catlin stared in amazement at the elegant young man in polished boots and good broadcloth who took his seat silently at the table. In silence Hannah reached out and rang the bell which would inform Non that they were ready to be served. It was not until the food had been brought in and Non had gone back to the kitchen that Hannah spoke.

"Has the top meadow been cleared?" she asked Alun.

"It has," affirmed Alun.

Thus it was during the rest of the meal, long silences, interposed with short questions concerning the farm from Hannah, and even shorter answers from Alun.

Catlin was completely bewildered by the strange atmosphere. She was shocked by Alun's appearance. She felt she would not have recognised him had she met him elsewhere. She wondered why he did not speak to her, or even look at her. Why did her mother dislike him so much? She must do so because it seemed as if she could hardly bear to speak to him. It was all so different from the daydreams she had indulged in at Castell Coed. She longed to escape from the imprisoning room and be by herself so she could think about these strange events and try to make sense of them. As soon as the meal ended she made the excuse of being tired from the journey in order to retire early. It seemed to her that Hannah accepted her excuse with relief. Alun continued to pay her no attention at all.

There was silence in the parlour for a while after she had left the room. Then Alun sprang to his feet with a string of Welsh oaths, knocking over his chair in his agitation. Not stopping to right it, he strode out of the room, slamming the door behind him.

Hannah was left alone at the white covered table with its clutter of uncleared dishes. She felt as if she was frozen into immobility. She was almost suffocating under the pressure of a confusion of emotions. Regret at her mishandling of the situation, concern for Catlin, a sense of humiliation, an impulse to weep wildly, but at the back of all this, wriggled a small serpent of rage that seemed likely to overcome all the others, given time.

'How dare he,' she fumed, 'behave as he has done!' To her, who had put the clothes on his back and who could throw him back into the world of vagrancy as easily as she had taken him out of it. It was the first time he had shown any signs of rebellion or dissatisfaction; he would have to be made to realise that it must be the last.

Hannah waited long in her room that night for Alun Ifans and when, at last, tired of waiting, she crossed the landing to his room, her gentle knock received no answer. Trying the handle she discovered the door was locked. She went back to her room. There was nothing more she could do tonight. To knock louder, to beat upon the locked door with clenched fists as she wanted to, would risk waking Catlin whose room was nearby.

'Tomorrow,' she thought, 'Tomorrow, I will change things. Catlin will have to be moved. I will put the fear of God into those gossiping servants. Alun will be brought to heel quickly enough. He must be. I promised myself this time, this time is mine and I will have it.' So she put all her confusion to flight and, in regained confidence of her control over the small world of Ty Garreg, went soundly and peacefully to sleep.

CHAPTER XV

Exhausted by the emotions of the previous day, Catlin slept late. It was past noon when she came down to find a household curiously serene after the tensions of the day before. The maids were working quietly and amiably in the kitchen. Nest, with tender enquiries about her health, set a bowl of creamy flummery before her. She was still eating it when Hannah came in. She too, appeared serene and pretty, in a lilac print dress with her hair looped softly round her ears. She teased Catlin about her late rising and told her gaily that she must finish her breakfast quickly as there was much work for them to do.

Vastly relieved at this change in her mother, Catlin quickly scraped the bowl clean and went eagerly to see what work there was to do. She was very surprised when Hannah called her along the corridor to tell her that she was to have a new room.

"You said you liked to have me near you!" she protested. "That is why I had the small room, and I like it, I like it very much. I have everything arranged so well in it."

"That can be done as well and better in a larger room, which is what you are to have now that you are such a grown girl that young men come courting you!"

"Oh, please, mother, I would so much rather not talk about it!" pleaded Catlin. But she was soon laughing, despite herself, as her mother skilfully changed the courtship of Emrys Hughes from the embarrassing and distressing episode it had been to her at the time, into something infinitely light and amusing.

But her face fell again as she looked at the long low room which had been her grandparents and which had not been entered since Evan Rees had lain injured in the high canopied bed. Hannah's face too, was momentarily grave as she realised how sombre the room was in contrast to Catlin's own sunny little chamber. Then, looking around, she saw how easily it could be brightened and then she positively whirled into action.

Trefor and a lad were summoned from the yard, the maids from the kitchen and the dark old room became a hive of activity. The old heavy pieces of furniture were banished to the attic. Carpet and hangings were earnestly discussed as to their suitability. The dark, heavy curtains, designed to keep out the light as well as the cold were discarded, but it was decided, somewhat doubtfully, that the carpet with its convoluted pattern of greens and browns would 'clean up well' and should be kept.

As the room began to empty, Catlin came to see its possibilities. The three tall narrow windows, released from the heavy hangings, now let in a good light and looked out on to a pretty, if limited, view of the orchard. There was an alcove into which her own small bed would fit neatly, leaving more room for her other pretty furniture. There was a large armoire of polished walnut which would hold all her dresses with ease.

"But what shall I do for curtains?" she asked anxiously, "The ones from my old room will not fit."

"Then you shall have new ones and covers to match," said Hannah. "Mrs Roberts can make them. I promised her some work a long time ago. And, perhaps, I really do not see why not, you shall have a new carpet as well! Tomorrow you and Mrs Roberts shall drive over to Newbridge and choose whatever is necessary from Mr. Howell's Emporium."

So Mrs Roberts was summoned to Ty Garreg and came there quickly and nervously, being still much in awe of Hannah. Catlin had been disappointed that Hannah was not going to accompany her to Newbridge but Mrs Robert's delight at the thought of such an expedition, at the idea of shopping so magnificently, even though it was for someone else, was so obvious that it made Catlin feel happy too. She now began to think that it was rather a grand thing to do - to be able to make one's own choice in such important matters.

Then began a very marathon of measuring and re-measuring, of checking and re-checking. Everyone, even Trefor, voiced their opinions as to what type of furnishing would be most fitting, and very conflicting most of these opinions were. But at last a list agreeable to all parties was compiled and a possible estimate of costs arrived at; the amount of which made Mrs Roberts almost swoon away.

As for the dark brown curtains and the dusty old carpet, they were given to Nest to dispose of as she thought fit. They were taken down to the big kitchen where Nest, with scrupulous fairness, divided them between Trefor for use in his own shabby cottage and Non for her mother's even poorer dwelling. The pleasure these gifts gave, the air of comfort, of opulence even, at least in the eyes of their new owners, that they bestowed on their homes for a long time to come, were more than Hannah in her careless generosity could ever have imagined.

CHAPTER XVI

The early mists still shrouded the fields as Catlin and Mrs Roberts set out next morning with the stable lad to drive them. The chill dampness clung to their clothes and wet their faces, but after a mile or so they left the mists behind and when they reached Newbridge they found its steep narrow streets bathed in sunlight. For hundreds of years, the little town perched above the estuary had remained more or less the same. But during the last fifty years or so it had changed a good deal. Small though it was, it had become the focal point of a wide area which contained, except for Castell Coed, no settlement larger than a village. Besides the weekly markets held there, it was also the place where services such as banking and medical and legal facilities could be found. Recently, a fair number of handsome houses had been built on the outskirts of the town by and for the more prosperous citizens. There were, however, others, like Gomer, who were more traditionally minded, and they still preferred to dwell in the tall, severe looking houses that stood in the centre of the town and had always housed the town gentry.

To cater for the increasing middle class as well as for the quite large numbers of country folk that came in from the surrounding countryside each market day, a large number of shops, many of them new, existed. Some of these establishments were rather grander than would have been expected by the casual visitor who was not aware of the town's importance to the area. So when Catlin entered the premises known as Mr Howell's Emporium, her entranced gaze met a blaze of colour from veritable barricades of carpets and from walls of shelves filled with a most dazzling display of furnishing materials.

Then began, for the two women, a time of great enjoyment. Mr Howell, himself volunteering to serve the 'daughter of Ty Garreg', sent his assistants scurrying from one end of the shop to the other, bringing him roll after roll of materials which he displayed upon the long polished counter with practised and impressive flourishes. The assistants, meanwhile, watched with some dismay as they calculated how long it would take to replace them on the shelves.

Catlin, with as much dignified composure as she could muster, and following the example of Mrs Roberts, most assiduously tested each sample for quality. She rubbed it between her fingers to estimate weight, scrunched it in her fists to decide its creasing properties, even sniffed at it to tell if the dyes had been properly absorbed. Finally, after much deliberation, and consultations with Mrs Roberts, she settled on a rosebud design, pinks against a creamy background. Then came the more important, more expensive business of choosing the carpet. To Catlin's delight she discovered a carpet which displayed not only rosebuds but full-blown roses as well!

Mr Howell, successfully concealing his jubilation at obtaining such a substantial order on a non-market day, swiftly calculated the cost of the goods, made a small deduction for own carriage and presented the total to Catlin. She was at first dismayed to find this sum exceeded the quite generous amount which Hannah had given her. Mr Howell, however, expressed himself as being more than willing to extend credit to such a valued customer and he soon persuaded Catlin easily, and Mrs Roberts, with more difficulty, that this would be the most sensible course to take, rather than returning another day or purchasing something that did not quite reach the standard of perfection of the preferred articles.

So it was settled, and leaving Mr Howell to arrange the packaging of the goods, Catlin set out to accompany Mrs Roberts as that lady made her own small purchases. Before they had left home Hannah had tried to persuade her daughter to visit her aunt and uncle but Catlin had been adamant in her refusal. She was not yet entirely convinced that her mother's light-hearted view of the Emrys Hughes affair was entirely the correct one and in any case she had no desire to meet that young man again for a while. Nor, indeed, had she any great desire to visit her Aunt Gwladys. In this, however, she was unfortunate, for as she emerged from the little draper's shop where Mrs Roberts had been selecting sewing cottons, she came face to face with her aunt.

One look at her aunt's face told Catlin that her instinct to avoid that lady had been the right one. Gwladys was very obviously not pleased to see her. Her grey, pebbly eyes were even harder, the lines surrounding her small pursed mouth carved even more deeply than usual in her plump fair face.

"Well, miss, what are you doing here?" she demanded. "Are you on your way to visit your uncle?" And as Catlin stumbled over answering both questions, she cried triumphantly, "I thought not! Indeed, I am not surprised you cannot face him, or me, or that poor lad you have so cruelly misled!" Stung by this, Catlin retorted that she had in no way ill-treated Emrys Hughes. That she had in no way invited his attentions.

"Did I say you had?" cried Gwladys. "No, I did not. It is your own conscience that put the words into your mind."

How long this public altercation would have continued, or what peak of intensity it would have reached it is difficult to say. For Mrs Roberts, an appalled witness, stood by wringing her hands, wishing to help Catlin but too nervous to intercede. Perhaps it was fortunate that at that moment Gomer joined them.

His normally mild expressioned face set in grim lines, as he addressed Gwladys in tones of suppressed fury.

"What now, wife! Are you and my niece going to stand here brawling like two common wenches for the entertainment of the rabble of Newbridge?" As Gwladys attempted to explain her grievance and enlist his sympathetic participation, he bade her brusquely 'be quiet', and grasping her firmly by the elbow with one hand, and Catlin as firmly by the hand with the other, turned them in the direction of Harbour Street and, as if in custody, led them homewards. Mrs Roberts, clutching her numerous small packages, followed unhappily after; not because she had the least desire to join in what was obviously a family quarrel, but simply because she did not know what else to do.

Once inside the wide heavy door which led into his hall, he propelled them towards the drawing room, pushed them inside and closed the door after them. Then turning to Mrs Roberts, he said courteously, "I am sure, Ma'am, you must be greatly fatigued. Let me find you a quiet place to rest." Having settled her comfortably in a small sitting room, he instructed a maid to take her a pot of tea. He then returned to the scene of battle.

Gomer caused for a moment outside the drawing room door. From inside he, heard the sound of raised voices. He took a deep breath and went in. He found Gwladys and Catlin in even fiercer confrontation than when he had first met them. A furious Gwladys whirled round to attack him.

"How dare you bring this shameless girl into my home!" she shrieked. "Have you no respect for my feelings?"

"This girl," replied Gomer quietly, "is my dead brother's only daughter and as long as I live she will have an honoured place in my house whatever she does. But come, tell me what great crime you believe her to be guilty of."

Then Gwladys told him, with much embellishment, how Catlin had slyly enchanted her nephew, luring him away from his own faithful sweetheart and then, after breaking up what would have been a fine match for him, had cruelly rejected his honourable proposal. Now he was pining for her to the extent of endangering his health.

"None of that is true!" burst out Catlin indignantly, no longer able to remain silent. "I had no wish to make Lettis unhappy, nor had I any wish for Emrys Hughes."

"But the fact is, my dear child," interposed Gomer mildly, "if my wife is to be believed, the fact is, that you do appear to have him. So what is to be done about it?"

"I don't know," wailed Catlin, "I want to go, to go home!"

"I cannot have you leave my house in this state," said Gomer firmly, "and I think it is important that I find out the truth of this matter." So saying, he rang the bell and told the girl who answered to send Mr Hughes to him immediately.

When that young man entered the drawing room, he was dismayed at the appearance of the little group which awaited him. There was his aunt, flushed and breathing stertorously. Catlin, not at all as he remembered her, equally flushed and, in her case, tearful. Above all, his employer looking very grim indeed. It was obvious to Emrys, who was no fool, that the events at Castell Coed, of which he had given his aunt a much edited account, must be the cause of this upset.

Gomer, fixing him with a stern eye, spoke first, "I hear, sir, that you have formed an attachment to this young lady. Tell me, and reflect carefully upon your answer, did she encourage you in any way to do this?" Before answering, Emrys looked from one to the other. Catlin avoided his gaze. His aunt's fierce eye for the moment encouraged him, but when he turned to speak to Gomer, the look upon that gentleman's face made him forget everything he had thought of saying in his defence and all he could mumble was,

"No, no, sir."

"That being the case," said Gomer, "you will probably agree that my niece did nothing to steal your affections away from your previous sweetheart?" Emrys, wishing fervently that he could be anywhere else other than in that confounded room, once more mumbled a negative. Shortly after, his wish was granted. For Gomer, after some stern words regarding the dangers of mischief making, sent him from the room.

As the door closed behind the crestfallen Emrys, Gomer spoke gravely to Gwladys. "It is obvious, wife, that you have been misinformed regarding this matter. It is now my earnest wish that you apologise to my niece and assure her of your future good intentions." Rather ungraciously, Gwladys complied with this directive and Catlin, with hardly more grace, accepted her grudging words of apology.

After a light meal, for her uncle had insisted on that, Catlin and Mrs Roberts returned to the Emporium to find that their purchases had been stowed away neatly in their wagon and all was ready for their journey home. As they jogged along the quiet road Catlin tried to revive her spirits by dwelling on the floral beauties of her new carpet and hangings. But she was not entirely successful in dismissing her aunt's bitter words from her mind. Again the doubt crept into her mind. Was she in any way responsible for Emrys behaviour and Lettis's resultant unhappiness? Also, now that the excitement of shopping had gone she felt some misgivings concerning her mother's reaction to the news that not only had she spent all the money she had given her but she was now in debt to Mr Howell's Emporium.

As for Mrs Roberts, she sat quietly going over in her mind the events of one of the most exciting days she had had for a long time. "Perhaps," she reflected, "with two such women as Hannah and Gwladys in the family, it was just as well that Aeros was not marrying into it!"

CHAPTER XVII

To Catlin's relief, Hannah received both the news of the extra cost and the encounter with Gwladys with equanimity. Indeed, the latter afforded her a good deal of amusement. She was pleased to hear how Gomer had stood so steadfastly by his niece. She had always got on well with her brother-in-law, admiring him for his learning and appreciating the grave courtesy with which he had always treated her. She had often wondered how he had come to choose Gwladys for his wife and had decided that it could only be explained as being one of those follies young men are prone to. As for Gwladys's treatment of Catlin, she added it to the long list of scores which she would one day settle with that lady.

For the next few days, Catlin was kept busy helping Mrs Roberts with the refurbishing of her new room. But the seamstress soon found she could do without her help, indeed preferred to, since this would extend her working time and consequently her wages. This unexpected windfall of paid work meant a great deal to the little woman. She had long been scheming for some way in which she could accumulate enough money to buy Aeros a new winter coat. His present one had grown pitifully threadbare.

Thus left to herself, Catlin began to find time hanging heavy on her hands. Although there had been no return to the strange behaviour which had greeted her in the kitchen when she had come home from Castell Coed, the old easy relationship with the servants had gone. She sensed a strange stiffness in their manner which she could only attribute to her mother's more formal attitude towards them. As for Alun, although she rode down to the beach several times, she never met him there. In fact, they seldom met at all, except at meal times, when his manner to her was always correct but curiously impersonal.

Once the matter of her change of room had been settled, Hannah made few demands on her, either for company or employment. In fact, she seemed often to find her mere presence rather a nuisance. It was Hannah, somewhat to Catlin's surprise, who reproached her for neglecting her school duties. Remembering what Lettis had said about Aeros Robert's attachment for her and her own subsequent romantic dreaming, made Catlin feel rather shy about meeting him again. It was, however, true what her mother had said. The school had been opened for some weeks now and she had totally neglected her duties there. And anyway, she was thoroughly bored with her own company. So the very next morning she put on her stoutest boots and walked across the dew drenched fields to Maesbach.

Aeros and the little ones were so obviously pleased to see her that she felt ashamed of her long absence. She saw more clearly than before that Aeros really had too much to do. It was an almost impossible task for him to keep the little ones gainfully occupied while at the same time trying to drill the basic elements of education into the heads of the big girls and boys who would soon be leaving their school days behind them and going out into the world to look for work. In a rush of emotion, engendered by a mixture of guilt and pity, Catlin promised that she would "come very, very often".

And so she did. But the duties, once found so pleasant, grew irksome. There were days when the schoolroom seemed cramped and dark (and so it was, with its windows set too high in its stone walls for the children to look out of) and the children lazy and stupid (and so some of them were). Aeros was often too busy to take notice of her, to see how pale and tired she was growing as she stood for long hours on the cold stone floor, trying to control her many small charges.

Then came the first really cold day of autumn. A north-easterly wind drove the fine, chilling rain almost horizontally across the bleak fields. The children sat huddled in their damp clothes, rubbing their red, cold hands together and staring sadly at the dead stove as if willing it into warm and cheerful life. Catlin asked why the stove had not been lit that morning and Aeros, intent on a piece of work, answered briefly that the winter allowance had not yet been delivered.

Catlin returned to her corner of the room without answering but became increasingly annoyed at the miserable conditions she was trying to work in. When she found that there were no materials left in the sewing cupboard for her needlework class she went again to Aeros. He reminded her that sewing materials had either to be provided by the girl's parents or donated by benevolent well-wishers.

Unfortunately, most of the girls' parents were extremely poor. The district had few wealthy and even fewer benevolent residents. Most parishes could have looked to the vicarage for assistance but the vicar here, besides being of a taciturn and parsimonious nature, was hardly better off than many of his parishioners. He did not hold the living in its entirety. The previous incumbent, although ill-health had obliged him to give up the duties of the parish and move elsewhere, was still alive and so entitled to a proportion of the stipend. The Reverend Williams had lost his only son at sea and his only daughter had recently been widowed. She had come home with her baby son to live with her parents and was almost wholly financially dependent upon them. She might have been interested in the school if she had had the time but, since her arrival home her mother had collapsed into semi-invalidism and the management of the vicarage as well as the care of her little son had fallen upon her shoulders.

Aeros' philosophical acceptance of the difficulties under which they were working infuriated Catlin (who was, at times, very much her mother's daughter). Without a word, she quite suddenly put on her cloak and bonnet and left the schoolroom.

Anger quickening her footsteps, she soon reached Ty Garreg where she found Hannah in the kitchen superintending jam making.

"Mother," she exploded, "you must send some coal down to the schoolhouse at once!"

Hannah looked up in surprise, her eyes narrowing at being so brusquely addressed. She told Catlin to follow her to the parlour. Once there she turned on her angrily, "How dare you speak thus to me, miss! Is it not enough that your father gave them the land, good land it was too, on which to build, and was forever paying for this and that? Is Ty Garreg to be drained for ever in order to pay for the schooling of a pack of peasant brats? Schooling which, in any event, will be of little value to them."

Shocked at this reception, Catlin's indignation and high resolve to remedy the situation at Maesbach dissolved into tears. Her obvious distress softened Hannah's heart and after a while she promised that a load of firing would be delivered to the school within the hour. Further than that, however, she would not go. Let others she said, remedy the other shortages of which Catlin complained.

Catlin, after leaving her mother, stood in the hall biting her lip and thinking of where she could get materials. She had some money in her room but no way of getting to Newbridge that day. Suddenly her face cleared and quickly and quietly she ran up the stairs to the linen cupboard. Unfortunately, as she came as quietly down the stairs, carrying with her a large and badly wrapped bundle, she met Hannah coming up. Hannah swiftly realised that the bundle she carried contained an assortment of her best embroidered linen sheets. For a moment she stared angrily at her daughter's flushed guilty face and then, with one of her quick changes of mood, she burst out laughing, "Oh, Catlin, what a goose you are! You cannot use those for pinafores. Come let us find something more appropriate."

Friends once more, mother and daughter happily ransacked cupboards and drawers until the extracted pile of materials grew too heavy for Catlin to carry. Then Hannah went to her own, now rarely used work basket, and tipped out a heap of bright silks and embroidery wool.

"Here, these will do for the big girls. Let them do something other than that eternal plain sewing!" Then she added a pair of most prettily made embroidery scissors and said, "Make these a prize for the best piece of work!"

Not content with this largesse, Hannah went to the kitchen and set Nest and Non busily scurrying about. So it was a triumphant Catlin that eventually returned to Ysgol Maesbach. Hannah, her mood for good works not yet exhausted, accompanied her. A load of coal and firewood had preceded them and tucked tidily into the gig they travelled in were not only the enormous pile of sewing materials but baskets of cakes as well as two large cans of creamy milk.

As Aeros looked around his schoolroom, now transformed by the light and warmth of a blazing fire, and saw his pupils laughing as they ate and drank, he mused on the strange enigma of Hannah Morgan. For a time, after their meeting in the churchyard, he had hated her for the hurt she had given to him and his mother. He had condemned her as a hard and cold woman. Lately, he had heard of even more disquieting news concerning her. Mrs Roberts, from her own observation as well as gossip from the servants, had soon realised that Mrs Morgan's relationship with her new farm manager was not all it should be. She had passed her observations on to her son who had been much distressed at the thought of Catlin being exposed to such moral contamination. Now as he watched mother and daughter happily unite in distributing the food they had brought and laughing and talking to the children, he became convinced that his mother had been misled by evil lying gossip and he resolved to take her to task that very evening.

During the next few weeks, Hannah's benevolent mood continued and her interest in the school encouraged others in the neighbourhood to show that it was not only the folk at Ty Garreg who were capable of generosity. So Aeros, somewhat to his bewilderment, soon found that Maesbach was fast becoming one of the best equipped little schools in the district. His pupils no longer had to struggle to write with squeaky pencils on cracked and faded slates. Nor did one battered textbook have to be shared between three or more. There were

books for all; even, and this was Hannah's doing, a pile of
brightly coloured picture books for the little ones who could not
yet read. These Aeros viewed with some misgivings. To his
mind, picture books for five year olds and embroidery for
twelve year olds were well enough for the children of the well-
to-do but valueless and even dangerous for boys who were
almost inevitably destined for the fields and quarries and their
sisters equally inevitably bound for domestic service. He
feared such innovations might encourage a frivolous attitude to
education and he knew too well from his own experience how
hard the road to learning was for a poor child. But he kept
these reservations to himself as he thanked Catlin and her
mother for all they had done.

His praise of her mother delighted Catlin. Far too often
lately, had she sensed criticism of Hannah from those around
her, and this had deeply distressed her. Now hearing Aeros,
whose opinion she greatly respected, praising her, enabled
Catlin to put her back on the pedestal which she had hitherto
occupied.

Despite the improved conditions at the school and a more
settled atmosphere at home, Catlin could not entirely recapture
her previous contentment. She often thought about Lettis and
wondered if her former friend's feelings were still as bitter
towards her. She was very thankful that she had never
confided to her those romantic dreams of Alun which had
occupied so much of her thoughts during her stay at Castell

Coed, for nowadays that young man seldom paid her any attention at all.

So her life continued in its slightly humdrum way until, when she least expected it (as is usually the case), there was an altogether unexpected event. Evan Rees came to call and brought Lettis with him. To Catlin's relief and surprise Lettis was forgiving, loving and ever so slightly condescending as she showed the sparkling ring on her left hand to her 'dearest friend'.

Emrys, wisely deciding after much contemplation, that a certain bird in the hand was worth infinitely more than an uncertain bird in the bushes, had returned to Castell Coed and sought the forgiveness and hand of Miss Lettis Rees. While declaring his undying affection he had given her a somewhat garbled account of the happenings at Gomer Morgan's home. From this, Lettis had somehow gained the impression that Catlin had sought Emrys out at her uncle's house but that he, having recovered from the indisposition and subsequent clouding of his judgement which he had suffered at Castell Coed, had rejected her in favour of his own true love, namely Lettis. Emrys, a little surprised at the interpretation Lettis had put on his confession did nothing to correct it, and so their reconciliation was complete. Evan, although not overjoyed at the prospect of Emrys as a son-in-law, reflected philosophically that Lettis might well have done worse. Now Lettis, in her new found dignity as an almost married woman, was more than willing to renew her friendship with Catlin, whom truth to tell she had sorely missed. She was, after all, the victor in what she saw as the battle for Emrys Rees, and it is always easy for the victorious to be magnanimous.

While the two girls, once more the best of friends, wandered arm in arm down to the paddock to say 'hallo' to Gracie, Evan visited Hannah. He found her much changed, although he could not quite say how. She had seemed pleased enough to see him but there was a brittle restlessness about her that worried him. He enquired as to Alun Ifan's progress in mastering the arts of farm management and she replied that he 'did very well'. But when he asked when he would be capable of taking over the estate, her answer was vague and despite his continued questioning, she could not be brought to a decision. Slightly exasperated, he abandoned the topic and instead brought her up to date with the progress being made on the new house but she seemed little interested in this. After a while they both sat in silence staring out of the window at the darkening sky.

Alun had been away at the market since early morning and was, therefore, unaware of the fact that there were visitors at Ty Garreg. Returning to the house he walked straight into the parlour without knocking, as was now his habit. He was startled to find Evan sitting there with Hannah. Evan looked up, equally started at the appearance of this tall, well-dressed young man who had so unceremoniously walked into Hannah's parlour.

For a moment he did not recognise him as Alun Ifans. It was not only the new clothes but the changes in his manner and expression. The smiling friendliness, the open honest countenance, had been replaced by a sulkiness, a look of petulant hauteur. When he spoke it was in English, spoken with a touch of Hannah's clipped tones, quite unlike the rolling lilt that Evan remembered.

The two men spoke for a while of generalities while Hannah sat silent between them, her head bent as she attentively studied her hands knotted together in her lap, as if they were something separate and strange to her. Only when Alun made to leave, saying he would intrude upon them no longer, did she raise her head and speaking softly tell him that 'there was no need to go, that she would order tea'. Alun ignored her invitation and after bidding Evan farewell, with chilling correctness, turned on his heel and left the room.

After he had gone, the room was silent, as Evan sat trying to make sense of what he had seen and heard. He found it difficult to reconcile his memories of the young sailor who had been his cheerful nurse companion with the arrogant man he had just seen dismiss Hannah's words as of no account. He now stared at Hannah and she stared back at him, lifting her chin and meeting his eyes with brave defiance, but the slow tide of colour rising from the collar of her neat dress betrayed her agitation.

Evan Rees was no fool. He realised, although he could hardly believe it, what the relationship between Hannah and her farm servant had become. He also realised that every social and moral law he lived by dictated that he leave the house and Hannah's presence immediately, but the awkward fact was, he did not want to. He had invested so much care, thought and emotion in the plans for their new life together. He could not bring himself to abandon them, to let it all go to waste. So they sat and talked of their future plans as if nothing had happened. Hannah spoke as if there was no doubt that the wedding would take place, although when, she could not be brought to say.

After a decent interval, Evan took his leave. He felt pale and shaken as if he had slid to the very edge of a precipice but by some good fortune had not gone over. Lettis, coming back to the house with Catlin, was surprised to find her father on the point of departure. He curtly dismissed her protests at the shortness of their visit and after a brief farewell to Catlin during which, somewhat to her mystification, he told her that if she ever needed a safe refuge she could find it with him, they were gone.

Hannah had gone back into the house without waiting to see them leave and now Catlin followed her.

"Is there something wrong?" she asked her mother. "What has happened?"

"Everything," answered Hannah cryptically, "or perhaps nothing. Time alone will tell." And time, she thought to herself, may well tell more than I would have it do.

CHAPTER XVIII

A few days later Hannah received a long letter from Evan Rees. Writing carefully and formally he told her how very much he wanted to marry her. He reminded her of the many plans they had made for their future together. He mentioned his daughter's approaching wedding and said how much help she would be to his motherless girl at that time. Then in the final paragraph he stated his terms. He would allow Hannah three months to arrange her business affairs and to decide if she really wanted to marry again. Beyond that, he would not go. Although it would cause him much distress, if they were not at the point of marriage in three months' time, he would regard their engagement as at an end.

For, he said frankly, he had made up his mind to find a wife and at his age he could not waste time pursuing a lost cause.

Hannah read and re-read the letter. Then she folded it carefully back into its envelope and sat staring down at it thoughtfully. Sighing, she rose and as she so often did in moments of crisis or indecision, went to her mirror.

"What shall I do girl?" she whispered to her reflection. "If I say 'yes' straight away would that be soon enough? But we could not marry tomorrow. There would be so much to arrange and even a few weeks' delay would be too long if what

I fear is true. But then, perhaps it is not and I am worrying for nothing. Best to leave things as they are for the time being?"

So she wrote back to Evan, saying that she accepted the time limit to her indecision and would give much thought to all he had said. Then, as relieved by this procrastination as if she had settled the problem, turned once more back to her obsessive love for Alun and her desire to see him entranced by her. But this, unhappily, he was not. Evan's visit had greatly upset him. He had thought to speak to him as a social equal, man to man; but this had not been achieved. Even their old friendly relationship was no more. Alun blamed this on Hannah. He shrewdly guessed that Evan understood how matters were between him and his employer and he believed that Evan now looked upon him with contempt as a betrayer of trust and a kept man - and in his heart he could not blame him for doing so.

It was in an effort to escape from such thoughts that Alun, ignoring all the work he had on hand, one afternoon took the familiar path down to the sea. After a night's heavy rain the path was dark with slippery mud but the air was soft and still. In the half-bare trees birds swung on branches and sang as piercingly sweet as if they thought spring had returned. Alun felt his spirits rise as he left the restraints of Ty Garreg behind him. He strode along, head thrown back and joined his own whistling to the birds' chorus.

It was not until he reached the rowan grove, where a few dried berries clung to leafless branches, that he realised he had been following Catlin. Her pony snickered a soft warning as she heard him approach and Catlin turned in the saddle to greet him. After a few words expressing their mutual surprise at meeting they continued down the twisting track in silence. Catlin keeping Gracie at a slow walk and Alun beside her keeping a steadying hand upon the mare's flank.

When they reached the beach, they sat as they had so often done earlier in the year, upon a little group of rocks and looked out at the sea. It was low tide and the brown wet sands stretched far before them to where the sea, colourless today under a cool sky, broke in tired little waves upon the shell strewn strand. A sea mist was slowly rolling in, and here there were no birds to break the stillness except for the occasional screech of a wheeling gull.

It was the first time they had been alone together since Catlin's last eventful visit to Castell Coed. Although Catlin had, as yet, no suspicion of Alun's affair with Hannah, she felt that much had changed since that time. The man sitting beside her seemed so much older than the still boyish young man who had confided his dreams to her. At first their conversation was stilted but soon Alun began to talk more freely and her diffidence too, disappeared. Within a short time they were chattering as happily together as they ever had.

They sat there up on the rocks until the lazy waters almost lapped their feet and the sea mist wrapped them round in it soft chilling embrace. Suddenly realising the threat of the approaching tide they scrambled laughingly to their feet and up the steep slope to the path above. As they climbed they held hands and when Alun kissed Catlin as he lifted her to the saddle it seemed as natural and inevitable as the rain that was now falling down softly upon them. By the time they reached the yard the fine shower had become a heavy downpour and Alun sent Catlin scurrying to the shelter of the house while he stabled her pony. Hannah caught Catlin running upstairs to change her clothes and scolded her for getting so wet and risking a chill, but she did not suspect that she had been with Alun.

It was not until he sat opposite the two women at dinner that night that the full realisation of his position dawned on Alun. He knew now that he loved Catlin. He also knew that at all costs he must keep the fact secret until he had had more time to think. His whole future still rested in Hannah's hands. So he kept his head bent low over his plate and spoke only in monosyllables throughout the meal.

But Catlin's eyes sparkled and her voice rang out so clearly as she excitedly described her afternoon's ride that he felt sure Hannah must suspect something soon even if Catlin did not, as appeared quite possible, trumpet forth the great news of her love to the entire household. Fortunately for him, Hannah's head ached and she soon bade Catlin to desist from her chatter and pay more attention to her plate.

As soon as he possibly could, Alun escaped from the parlour. Closing the door behind him, he drew a deep breath

of relief and momentarily cursing all women he went swiftly
out to the barns. He felt that for tonight, and perhaps for a
good many nights to come, the companionship of dumb beasts
would be safer than that of the ladies of Ty Garreg.

But Alun seldom took notice of wise counsel, even his own.
The next afternoon, and many following, he spent on the beach
with Catlin. He had managed to persuade her that, for the time
being, their love should be secret. He told her that when he
had saved enough money he would carry her away to that little
white house by the sea where they would live in happiness for
ever after. Indeed, at the time he was saying it, Alun himself
believed in the sweet future he so vividly described to her. As
he went about his daily work he imagined Catlin, a white apron
tied neatly round her slender waist, making all tidy in the little
house as she waited for him to sail into harbour. He imagined
his business prospering, children growing up around them, and
the two of them becoming as respected a couple as ever lived
along that rocky coast.

While, unknown to Hannah, their autumn idyll continued,
she herself was becoming increasingly distraught. Although,
still not suspecting Catlin to be the cause, she sensed she was
losing whatever hold she had ever had over her young lover.
Desperately she sought for ways to keep him attracted, to keep
him near her, but he constantly made work an excuse to be
away from the house. He now began to pester her for money,
complaining that although he was doing a farm manager's work

he was still being paid a labourer's wage. Afraid of making him independent she gave him as small an increase as she dared but still it was enough to allow him to start a small savings fund. At first, this gave him great satisfaction, but when he calculated how long it would take him at the present rate to save enough to buy a boat, his dissatisfaction returned.

His determination to break with the widow, as he now called her to himself, strengthened. As did his resolution to win Catlin. His courtship increased in ardour, half-frightening, half-delighting the girl. She longed to confide and share their plans with her mother but was deterred from doing so by Alun's warnings that Hannah would only try to separate them because he was still a poor man.

CHAPTER XIX

It was during this period of strained relationships that Hannah had at last to admit to herself that even if she had wanted to marry Evan Rees it was no longer possible for her to do so. The only way she could think of to save herself and her family from widespread scandal and disgrace was to persuade Alun Ifans to marry her immediately. At first she tried to conceal from him her reason for wanting a speedy marriage but his sullen reception of her proposal at last drove her to disclose her secret.

Alun's reaction to the news of his rapidly approaching fatherhood was far from enthusiastic. He was at first shocked, then outraged. He accused Hannah of setting a trap for him, of planning the event from the beginning. He told her he wanted nothing more to do with her.

At this, Hannah lost her temper and threatened that if she was to be disgraced then she would make certain that she was not the only one to suffer. She would make known his behaviour far and wide. She would ensure that no-one offered him respectable employment for miles around. Alun knew that this was no idle threat and that she could do this and more. While the fathering of an illegitimate child was not in itself so unusual an occurrence in the countryside as to necessarily make him a social outcast, the circumstances of this liaison were sufficiently extraordinary as to cause a greater scandal than he could comfortably live with. So he controlled his fury and set about placating her as best he could. He told her that the shock of the news had greatly unsettled him, made him say things that she must know he did not mean. "Within a few days," he said, "we shall see all settled."

Nevertheless, it was in a black and furious mood that he went to keep his appointment with Catlin that afternoon. He felt like a trapped animal that, despite its twistings and turnings, could find no escape from its prison. In fact, he was imprisoned, shackled by his obsessive desire to own a boat and to be a man of substance in his village. Of course, he could have simply walked away from Ty Garreg, a free man, but then he would have been nothing more than a penniless traveller again. He could, of course, marry Hannah but this would tie him forever to the land. And what of Catlin? She added yet another strand to the tangle.

Catlin was already on the beach when he arrived and ran happily to meet him. As she drew near she was startled by the drawn expression on his face.

"What has happened?" she asked. "Why do you look so sad and angry?"

Alun stood silent for a moment, then on an impulse he said, "There is only one thing to do, I must go away, there is nothing else I can do!" She burst into frightened tears and as he held her sobbing against his shoulder he found himself falling into a role; playing a part in which he half-believed.

"It will only be for a short time, Catlin. I shall get everything ready and then I shall send for you. Oh, truly we shall have a fine life, then." He took from the small finger of his left hand a battered silver ring. He had won it in a dice game and worn it ever since in the belief that it brought him luck.

"Wear this for me, dear love. One day soon I will replace it with pure gold!" he said. Almost overcome with emotion, Catlin tugged off the garnet ring Hannah had given her. She gave it to Alun asking him to wear it in memory of her until they should meet again. They stayed together on the beach exchanging vows and plans for the future until it was almost too dark to see each other and then they walked home hand in hand through the deep shadowy lane, the faithful Gracie clip-clopping slowly along behind them.

However, once Alun was back in his room at Ty Garreg he quickly forgot his play-acting (if that was all it had been) and settled down to making some serious plans. His immediate need was for money - large amounts of it. He considered that the satisfaction of this need was no more than his rightful due. For had he not worked hard and long for it? His only source of money was Hannah and the simplest way of getting it was to marry her. But this he was determined not to do. He did not altogether discard the idea of marrying Catlin. However, he had not the slightest idea how the difficulties this would cause could be overcome.

When he went to Hannah's room that night, he told her that he would certainly marry her as soon as possible. But she must realise that gossip would then make it impossible for them to continue living at Ty Garreg. To Hannah's startled question as to what else they could do, he answered that they could go and live in his village. She then heard for the first time of his dream of owning a small coastal vessel, for by now his ambitions had progressed beyond a mere fishing boat. He explained that they could live quite comfortably on the proceeds of his voyaging and that within a few years her style of life would compare favourably with what she had now. But first he must find some capital. He would have to buy a craft and the first cargo, unless he could get a commission straight away. They would also have to have somewhere to live.

Hannah, her head in a whirl, asked how much all this would cost. She was appalled at the size of the sum he named.

"Where can I find so much money?" she demanded angrily. "Do you think I keep crocks of gold under my bed?"

Alun looked at her in surprise and then speaking slowly and patiently as if to a particularly stupid child said, "But of course, you will have to sell this place!"

"Sell Ty Garreg?" cried Hannah angrily, "you loon, it is not mine to sell!"

"Then whose it?" asked Alun in amazement.

"It is my sons'."

"But you are their mother!"

"Oh, God!" said Hannah, "Do you not understand? It is entailed upon them!" Seeing that Alun was still mystified, she proceeded to explain the workings of the law as it applied to the inheritance of Ty Garreg.

It was a much crestfallen Alun who was finally brought to understand that Hannah was not quite the fabulously wealthy independent woman he had believed her to be. He still sulkily insisted that his plan for their marriage was the only viable one and in her heart Hannah had to agree with him. She had no wish to face a life of social ostracism, nor had she any illusions as to her capacity to endure a life of 'love in a cottage'. So she told Alun that within the next few days she would see what could be done to raise the necessary money to start them off in a new way of life.

Seeing, however, no advantage in delay, she was up betimes the next day to prepare for the journey to Newbridge. As a trustee of her husband's will, Gomer would have to be consulted should she attempt to raise a loan using Ty Garreg as security. Really, she hoped to persuade him to arrange the whole matter for her. She had always suspected that he had a liking for her. Now was the time for her to take as much advantage of their friendship as she was able.

To her great disappointment Gomer was neither so affectionate nor as helpful as she had hoped for. In fact, he looked in horror at his sister-in-law, sitting there so demurely in her dark cloak and bonnet.

"You wish to mortgage Ty Garreg? You cannot mean it. It is your children's inheritance, left to you in sacred trust. It is their home. It is your home."

"After my marriage to Mr Rees," said Hannah quietly, "it will no longer be my home, or theirs. My sons' future may well lie elsewhere. Like you, they may not be drawn to a farming life. Above all, I feel that it is unreasonable for me to expect my future husband to accept the responsibility of a property that may well come to be a drain on his income!"

"That is nonsense," exclaimed Gomer angrily, "Ty Garreg will never be a drain. On the contrary, it will provide you all with a most useful income for years to come. As for whether my nephews will wish to farm there or not, that will be for them to decide when they come of age. I tell you frankly, sister-in-law, I will not allow you to endanger their futures. I must also warn you that the entail stands firm in law; it can only be broken by their death - which God forbid."

Shocked by his anger, Hannah burst into tears. Indeed there seemed nothing else for her to do, "I need the money!" she sobbed, "Indeed I must have it!"

Gomer became more alarmed than ever. He had never imagined that he would ever see the normally composed Hannah behaving like any ordinary hysterical woman. There must be some very serious cause behind all this.

"Tell me," he asked soothingly, "Why do you need so much money? Evan Rees is a prosperous man and a sensible and generous one. I cannot believe that he would encourage you in such folly."

But Hannah would not explain herself further, only reiterated her demand that he must help her obtain a large sum of money. Finally to placate her and to stop her going elsewhere for advice, he promised to see what he could do to help her obtain a loan using Ty Garreg as security.

Refusing an invitation to dine, Hannah bade Gomer a quiet farewell. She felt very much alone as she climbed the short hill which led into the High Street. When she reached it she stood still on the pavement, looking from right to left, hardly knowing what to do. The interview with Gomer seemed to have drained her of all emotion. It was market day and the street was crowded with country folk. She felt calm, completely isolated from the day to day preoccupations of the passers-by who pushed and jostled around her. She placed no reliance on her brother-in-law's promises. She saw clearly enough that he was merely humouring her. The fact was - and she had to face it - that while her sons lived she was nothing but a pensioner living on the bounty of Ty Garreg.

She recovered herself a little and crossed the street to avoid a group of drunken carters. She found herself opposite a large chemist's shop, its windows filled with jars of brightly coloured liquids and various advertisements. With no clear idea of what she wanted she entered the shop and idly walked around surveying the packages of soap and various beauty aids. Gradually she became aware of a low-toned conversation being carried on between the chemist and a brisk little woman, tidily dressed in a striped woollen skirt and a neat shawl.

"I have told you before, Mrs Evans, that you must be extremely careful with this medicine. It was only last week that I sold you a large bottle and here you are back again."

"What would you have me do, then?" asked the woman. "Should I leave the poor soul to suffer? You know well, Mr. Morris, that she has very little time left."

"Indeed, yes," sighed the chemist. "Very well, then. You shall have some more. But do try to make it last a little longer this time, Mrs Evans."

After the woman had left the shop, Hannah approached the counter. "What was the medicine you sold that woman?" she asked. The chemist looked at her keenly, then reassured by her air of respectability and prosperity answered. "It was laudanum, a great gift against pain and suffering if used with care, but a great danger in the hands of the careless."

"Could I use it against the toothache?" queried Hannah. "For I and my daughter constantly suffer from that affliction!"

"Indeed you could," answered the chemist.

As Hannah left the shop, the bottle of laudanum concealed in her reticule, she saw the Revd. Williams and his daughter approaching. Yielding to an impulse to avoid them, Hannah turned quickly to her left down a narrow side lane and then right and then left again. In an effort to find her way back to the High Street she went into an alley which ended in a small court where tiny cottages huddled together in the shade of a towering stone wall. Two emaciated dogs ran baying at her and she hastily retraced her steps. The path she now followed seemed to lead steadily downhill.

This was an area of Newbridge she had hardly known existed. The tall grey buildings had given way to small rough stone cottages and now the path came to an abrupt end on an area of muddy foreshore dotted here and there with clumps of wiry grass. Beyond this lay the river, sluggish with rubbish and debris of all kinds. Behind her and on either side, making an open square, were rows of mud-walled, one-roomed dwellings, their poorly-thatched roofs looking as incapable of keeping out the rain as their cracked and sagging doors of keeping out the wind.

The place was alive with bare-foot children who stopped their games to stare at the well-dressed stranger. Slatternly women, alerted by the unusual silence, came to their doors to see what was the cause of it. Hannah became uncomfortably aware that she was the focus of a generally hostile attention. One woman, in particular, black hair tangled above keen black eyes, stared in fascination at the hem of Hannah's skirt which she had slightly raised to avoid the mud. The raised hem revealed a flounce of white petticoats which bloomed incongruously white and pure against the garbage strewn earth. What lay behind the woman's fascinated gaze Hannah could only guess. Perhaps she was calculating that the cost of one such piece of finery would keep her in food for months. Or perhaps the sight had simply revived her feminine longing for such adornment. Whatever it was, the mood was soon broken.

A small child, trying out her first uncertain steps, stumbled across to Hannah, tripped at the last moment and clutched at her skirts for support, then looked up crowing with delight at her achievement. Instinctively, Hannah's hands went out to steady her, filthy and muddy as the child was. But as she held her, the staring woman was transformed into a protective virago, rushed across and snatched the child from her. Back in the safety of her doorway, she launched a tirade of abuse in language Hannah could hardly understand. Encouraged by this antagonism, an urchin picked up a handful of mud and threw it at Hannah. As the filth spattered itself across her bodice, Hannah in sudden terror ran from the place. Without any thought as to direction, she ran through one small street after another, until she found herself standing on the old stone bridge that spanned the river.

Hannah lent upon the sturdy parapet and took deep breaths of the damp, cold air. The place she had run from, with its atmosphere of poverty and degradation, had filled her with horror. But the most horrifying fact of all, the one that kept beating at her brain defeating all her attempts to ignore it, was that those nightmarish creatures had similarly found something in her that caused them to hate and despise her. What had they seen in her, what did they know, that had made them feel so? Would it not have been more normal for them to cringe and beg?

There was a din of hammering and thumping coming from the many small workshops that crowded together at the far end of the bridge. The noise seemed to hang in the air and vibrate in her brain. With trembling hands she opened her bag to search for a handkerchief. Her eyes fell on the neatly wrapped package she had brought from the chemist's shop. She took it out and stood weighing its cool smooth shape in her gloved hands, then with a quick, almost reflex action she hurled it into the river. She had expected it would smash or sink but it bobbed and weaved as if seeking its way and then, floated downstream to where the small ships were busily discharging their cargoes of lime and coal.

Calmed by her action and conscious of a deep exhaustion such as she had never known before, Hannah left the bridge and started to climb the steep hill that led up into the centre of the town. Halfway up she was forced to stop and lean for support against the windowsill of a small house. Half-fainting, she became aware of a woman's concerned voice asking if she would not come in and rest. Thankfully she accepted the proffered arm and allowed herself to be led into the house.

Within a few minutes she was sufficiently recovered to be able to look around her. She was seated in a small neat parlour which contained a few small tables and several chairs. She realised that she was in the house of one of those enterprising housewives who on market days turned their homes into modest places of refreshment. Thereby, providing a service for the womenfolk of farmers who might find themselves temporarily abandoned while their men conducted their business in the markets and public houses. Fortunately for Hannah, there were no other customers and the landlady was happy to fuss over the well-dressed but obviously distressed woman she had found on her doorstep.

Within a short time, the fire had been coaxed into a blaze and the tiny table supported a plate of Welsh cakes and a pot of steaming tea. Hannah thought she had never tasted tea so good or experienced such a feeling of safety and peace as she did in that small homely room. She wished that time would stand still so that she might stay forever sipping tea and warming her feet by the comforting blaze.

Her contentment did not last long. Her hostess returned and now her questions revealed not only kindness but a natural curiosity. "It is only that I walked too far, took a wrong turning and found myself in an unfamiliar part of the town," Hannah told her. She rose and quickly gathered together her belongings. She bade the woman good-bye, left her more money than she need have done, and then stepped out into the gathering dusk.

Refreshed, and her strength restored, the nightmarish strangeness of the streets had vanished and Hannah quickly found her way back to the town centre. There she met up with Bryn who had been searching, as he said, "All over Newbridge for her!" They were soon on their way home, delayed only by Hannah's insistence that they stop at a confections shop. There she bought toffee for Thomas and Owen and a box of sugared almonds for Catlin who was inordinately fond of them. Then snugly wrapped in a warm rug, she drove thankfully homewards, feeling as if she had escaped from some great and terrible danger.

CHAPTER XX

As usual, Hannah slept soundly that night and woke much refreshed. She had not yet spoken to Alun concerning her visit to Newbridge, but appraising her serene looks and manner he could only suppose that her business talks had gone well. After breakfast Ianto came to see him, complaining that several water courses had become clogged with mud and leaves and were threatening to flood. Glad of an excuse to leave the house, Alun ordered that some of the men working in the yard be switched to clearing the drains and he himself went out to supervise the work.

Catlin and the boys had already left for school and so Hannah found herself alone except for the maids who were busy about their own work. She went into the parlour (her familiar refuge) and sitting at her small desk drew out the folder which contained the records of such savings and readily cashable securities as she possessed. At the end of an hour she had made a fair estimate of how much money she could lay her hands on within a week or so. It was not as much as she had hoped. Some of the rents had not yet come in and some of those, she knew from past experience, would not be paid except under extreme pressure and she did not have the time for that.

Ironically, this year, a larger than normal share of the profits had been ploughed back into the estate. Much of this had been done at Alun's request. He had reported to her the need, as he saw it, for many repairs as well as for some new buildings. Hannah, glad to see him taking an interest in the place, had given him more or less a free hand to undertake such improvements as he thought necessary. She now noted sourly that even 'that great lump Trefor' had benefited from this general largesse to the extent of a new roof.

She sighed as she surveyed the results of her calculations. There was not nearly enough money to set Alun up as he desired. Even handled with care it would only serve to keep them in moderate comfort for a year or two. And what then of Thomas, Owen and Catlin? With some dismay, she realised that until now she had hardly included them at all in her plans, but, of course, they had to be. If she went away with Alun, giving him what money she had, how could she carry out her plans for the boys' schooling; and what of Catlin? How little she had thought of the girl lately. It was not that her great attachment for her had diminished, only that it had, as it were, been put into storage until easier times should come again. Now the problem of Catlin's probably unfavourable reaction to her mother's marriage to Alun Ifans and their subsequent removal from Ty Garreg had to be faced. Hannah buried her head in her hands. It seemed to her that no sooner had she come to face with a fair degree of equanimity one chasm of calamity in her life, than before her eyes yawned another.

Her reverie was broken by Non coming in to announce a visitor. Gomer, in an attempt to gain time, had sent Emrys over with a sheaf of papers for Hannah to look through. These were, in fact, of no great importance but he hoped they would keep her occupied for long enough to allow him time to consult with Evan Rees.

The arrival of a messenger from Gomer, and moreover one carrying so many official looking papers, cheered Hannah considerably. In a mood to clutch at any straw, she told herself that she had been too quick to despair. She must surely have misjudged Gomer. Quite obviously he meant to help her and was only being his usual careful, cautious self. She looked at Emrys with a kindliness born of her new hope. Had there not been some talk of a liking on his part for Catlin? She could not quite remember the details of it; her mind had been so clouded lately, but surely it had been so. He deserved a reward for bringing such good news and perhaps it would please Catlin too, to see an old admirer. So Emrys was despatched to Maesbach to tell Catlin that her mother needed her at home.

Emrys had been most unwilling to visit Ty Garreg but had been unable to find an excuse for refusing. He was now just as unwilling to fulfil Hannah's request, but again, could find no way in which to refuse the task. As he walked across the fields he reflected gloomily that this was the last place in the world he wanted to be and Catlin definitely the last person he wanted to see. He also told himself that he was sick of being treated as an errand boy.

However, as he trudged lugubriously through the water logged meadows he came upon a group of men up to their knees in muddy water as they dredged out a ditch. Most perversely, the scene cheered him and soothed his hurt pride. After all, he reflected as he compared their appearance with his, he was already in a much better position than many young men of his age and was bound to do even better in the future.

It was, therefore, a rather self-satisfied young man who called at the schoolhouse to take Catlin home. She, although rather flustered at meeting Emrys again so unexpectedly, came willingly enough when she heard Hannah's message. At first she feared that the summons may have been caused by some kind of emergency but Emrys told her that, as far as he could tell, Hannah was in good health. Nor, as far as he could see, had any disaster, natural or otherwise, befallen the house or its inmates. So Catlin accepted that it was simply one of Hannah's whims. She sighed a little as she thought to herself that her mother would never see her work at the school as anything more than a way of passing the time and she knew that she was quite capable of calling her away simply to pour tea or perform some similar routine task.

The discussions about the reasons for the summons home had helped to bridge the first awkward moments between

Emrys and Catlin. Now they continued to chat fairly easily about the school, the weather and other general topics. However, when their interest in these topics were exhausted, Catlin decided they could no longer ignore the subject that was surely uppermost in both their minds.

She stopped and fixing Emrys with her large serious eyes, said, "Lettis has told me that you and she are to be married. I want to tell you how happy that makes me and that I hope we shall all continue to be friends."

Emrys looked back at her, meaning to accept her congratulations with dignity, but suddenly all his self-satisfaction melted away and he put out his hand in an almost pleading gesture and said softly, so softly she could hardly hear him, "Oh Catlin, I wish it could have been you!"

They completed the rest of the short journey in silence and Hannah was surprised at the solemnity of the two young people as they came in. However, in her present mood she could not imagine that anyone else could have problems in any way comparable to the seriousness of hers and so dismissed them from her mind. When Catlin asked the reason for her summons home she merely answered, "No reason, dear girl, except that I was missing you!" Catlin, long used to her mother's oblivion to all interests except her own, accepted this reasoning with her usual good humour.

After a light meal, Emrys set off on his journey back to Newbridge, carrying with him a letter from Hannah thanking

Gomer for what he had already done and reminding him of the urgency of her need. However, when Emrys arrived at the solicitor's home he was not there. For as soon as his business commitments had permitted he had ridden over to Castell Coed to consult with Evan Rees.

As he had suspected, Evan knew nothing of Hannah's plan to either sell or mortgage Ty Garreg and his face grew increasingly grave as he listened to Gomer's tale. When it was finished he sat in silence for so long that Gomer became anxious, fearing that he had perhaps misjudged the situation and that maybe Evan was involved in this money raising venture of Hannah's. But Evan's silence was because, for the moment, he was completely lost in his own thoughts. He had been deeply affected, although not completely surprised by what Gomer had told him. Whatever Hannah's reasons for her actions were (and he could only guess that they were connected with Alun Ifans) they showed plainly enough that she had finally rejected him as a suitor. He was rather surprised at the amount of pain this knowledge caused him.

Then becoming aware and taking pity on Gomer's obvious unease, he pulled himself out of his reverie and said to him,

"I do hope, Mr. Morgan, that you will believe me when I tell you that I have had no hand in this. I confess that when I first met the lady her comfortable circumstances had some influence upon forming my attachment for her. As you know, I have a reasonably good income of my own, but my plans for the future might well involve expenditure on such a level as to cause some strain on my present resources. However, I have come to value her mind and person so much that I would willingly take her without a penny. Now I very much fear that some trouble has come upon her. Unfortunately, she has neither confided in me nor sought my help in any way, so there is really nothing I can do. But please be assured that if there is any way in which I can help her, I will not hesitate to do so."

With these assurances, Gomer had to be content. He rode back to Newbridge an extremely worried man. He bitterly regretted the fact that if his sister-in-law must give up her comfortable widowhood (and for his part he could see no reason why she should) she should have been such a fool as to reject an eminently well-qualified suitor like Evan Rees. He had always regarded Hannah as a sensible woman. What on earth could have happened to change her into the wholly irrational creature he now had to deal with. He could only suppose that it was caused by a delayed reaction to the shock of her husband's death. At the thought his face softened and he resolved that, however foolish and irresponsible she became, he would continue to help her as best he could for his dead brother's sake.

He had not told Gwladys of Hannah's request but he wondered whether the time had now come when he should. Perhaps a woman's influence might help restore Hannah's sanity. But even as he thought this, he had to reject the concept. Even Gwladys's husband had to acknowledge that the picture of her acting as a ministering angel to Hannah was quite ludicrous as well as most unlikely. He sighed deeply. It would have to be him or no one at all. He decided to postpone action for the next few days. A procedure which had often worked wonders for him in the past in all sorts of difficult situations.

Unfortunately, it was not a procedure that had ever particularly appealed to Hannah and during the next few days she became increasingly impatient as she waited in vain for a communication from Gomer. Then something happened that made her realise afresh how truly desperate her situation was.

On one of those surprisingly calm and gentle days that, in that part of the country in late autumn interposed with days of wild winds and heavy rain, Catlin and Alun lay beneath a hedge bordering the rowan grove. These days Catlin hardly needed to ride Gracie down to the sea as a pretext for meeting Alun. For Hannah seldom bothered to question her regarding her activities, supposing that if she were not at home she must be down at the school. Of late, however, Catlin had spent little time at Maesbach, preferring to spend her afternoons wandering along the beach and cliffs in the hope of meeting Alun. If the weather was so bad as to make this unlikely she would instead sit in her room dreaming of a seascaped future. Today, however, had not been one of lonely dreaming and disappointment, for she had not yet reached the beach when she met Alun on his way back. Now they lay in each other's arms, sheltered from the wind and as they thought, from the gaze of passers-by.

Thus, they were discovered by Aeros Roberts. It was the day of the annual hiring fair in Newbridge. So many children had stayed away so as to be able to accompany their parents to the fair that the school had been depleted of more than two thirds of its scholars. The high-ceilinged school room seemed more than usually dreary that day. Outside the sun shone brightly but except for a very short period it was unable to send its rays through the narrow high-set windows. At last, Aeros took pity on his forlorn little group of loyal pupils and declared a half-holiday.

The children, on hearing this welcome news, made off as fast as they could, scattering to their cottage homes like a flock of starlings. There they would pester and worry their mothers to let them go to the fair like their more fortunate fellows. For not only was this the day when servants of all descriptions would fill the town square hoping to find the perfect employer - he who would ask little and pay much - but it was also the day when traders, some from a great distance away, would have come into the town and set up their stalls. By ten in the morning both sides of the High Street would be lined with stalls piled high with every variety of goods one could think of. Latecomers would have to content themselves with finding a vacant slot in one of the narrow side streets. By early afternoon the town would be packed from end to end with eager

152

shoppers looking for bargains, as well as those who just came to look and stare.

Needless to say, buyer and bargain met as seldom as perfect servant and perfect master, but enough new hirings of a satisfactory kind were made and enough good bargains found, or thought to be so, as to make the matter of celebration imperative. So by evening the many small taverns the town boasted would be crowded to bursting point. As the night wore on, there would be more brawling and roistering in Newbridge than on all the other nights of the year put together.

It was this rowdy aspect of Fair Day that made Aeros reluctant to visit the town that day. But neither was he drawn to the pile of school work that waited to be done. He decided that he too would have a holiday. He had long intended to explore a certain cliff path of whose beauties and dangers he had heard much. So after persuading his mother to pack him a light meal and listening patiently to her many words of warning and advice, he set off in a happy mood of adventure and holiday.

From the back of the school house a narrow path led somewhat precariously downhill to the rowan grove that grew above the beach. It was thus, coming from behind the trees, that he stumbled upon the two lovers. At first he made to turn away in simple embarrassment then he saw to his amazement that the girl was Catlin and the man who was her mother's farm bailiff. The shock of finding Catlin, whom he had near worshipped, in such a compromising situation was almost more than he could bear. His mother's words came back to him, along with other whispered scraps of gossip and sniggering that had come to his ears regarding the red-haired sailor and the lady of Ty Garreg. Now his fury fell on Alun as both the despoiler of innocence and the destroyer of his own dreams.

Alun had by now scrambled to his feet and stood staring in some puzzlement at the schoolmaster, whom he knew by sight. He was wondering why the devil the fellow did not have the tact and good sense to simply move on. He was further astonished by 'the fellow' rushing at him and raining blows on his undefended head and body. Taken by surprise, he was knocked to the ground and Aeros for a moment thought he was the victor. But the sailor had been toughened by years of brawling in portside bars and he soon showed the schoolmaster that he was no match for him. In another few minutes it was Aeros who lay stretched upon the ground.

Alun, by now enraged at what he saw as a totally unprovoked attack upon him, kicked viciously at his opponent's head and body. At this Catlin, who had been crouching against the hedge staring in disbelief at the battling figures, cried out to him to stop. When her cries had no effect she rushed forward and flung herself across the schoolmaster's unconscious body. Alun tried to prise her away from him, but she clung to Aeros with all her strength, shielding his bruised and bloody head against her breast.

Beside himself with rage and disgust, Alun screamed at her, "Stay there then, you fool. All you Ty Garreg women are the same. You take a man, you twist him, you make him something else!" Then, his rage suddenly abating, he stared down at the man and girl crouched on the muddy ground and added in a calmer tone, "I tell you, before I came here, I was not as I am, and what I am now I scarcely know!"

As he ran from them, Catlin heard his heavy boots clattering and skidding on the stony track. She listened until the sounds disappeared then took out her handkerchief and wiped the blood as best she could from Aeros's face. His eyes remained closed and blood continued to bubble from his nose but she knew from the raucous sound of his breathing that at least he still lived. She sat there upon the cold, damp grass, cradling his head in her lap and thought, 'What will become of us all if he dies?'

CHAPTER XXI

Happily, Aeros did not die. His injuries were not as fearful as the profuse flow of blood from his nose and the cuts around his eyes made them appear. Once he had regained consciousness he was soon able to stand and with Catlin's help make his way home.

Catlin knew that she would remember for ever that journey across the fields to the schoolhouse. The brief winter sun had gone and the cold mists were rolling in from the sea. Needing both hands to support Aeros, she had to let her skirts trail in the damp grass. They soon became soaking wet and their weight was a further burden to her. As they stumbled along the overgrown track Aeros did not speak to her or she to him. The only sound on the still air was the rasp of his breathing as he struggled to cope with the pain of his broken ribs where Alun's boots had found an easy target.

When at last they arrived at the schoolhouse they both fell exhausted against the door. It was Catlin who finally found the strength to try the door and finding it locked beat her fists against the panels hysterically, crying out to Mrs Roberts to let them in. As the door opened, Aeros, released from Catlin's grasp, fell in across the doorstep, and lay at his mother's feet.

It was now that Mrs Roberts showed the steel beneath her frail exterior. After her first startled shriek of horror, she wasted no time on further hysterics. With an almost superhuman effort she managed to drag her son down the little hall to the kitchen, where a rag rug lay in front of the fire. When she had placed a cushion beneath his head and removed his boots she proceeded to deal with his injuries as best she could. Only when she had done everything she possibly could did she turn her attention to Catlin.

All this time the girl had stood, half-supported by the scrubbed kitchen table, her head hanging low on her breast. When Mrs. Roberts spoke to her she did not answer, she hardly seemed to hear. Looking closely at her the woman decided she had no serious injury, if any, and taking her by the shoulders she shook her into some kind of activity. Together they managed to lift the now conscious Aeros to a chair. She then pushed Catlin into another and gave them both some of the soup which had been simmering on the fire. Not until she saw some colour creeping back into their cheeks did the sensible little woman begin to ask questions.

Catlin did not answer her but looked appealingly towards Aeros. "Oh Mam," he gasped, breathing painfully because of his damaged rib, "don't fuss now. It was an accident. I fell from the rocks and Catlin found me. She helped me home!" Mrs Roberts opened her mouth to question him more closely but seeing the pallor creeping back again across her son's face, shut it again. Now was not the time to burden him with questions he obviously did not want to answer. She must somehow get a doctor to him, but how was that to be done?

She turned her attention to Catlin once more. The girl was pale and obviously exhausted. Her skirt was wet and mud-stained but she appeared to have no cuts or bruises, although blood streaked her face and hands. She pulled the girl to her feet and speaking very slowly and clearly as to a sleepy child said, "Go home now as fast as you can. See that word is sent for a doctor to visit my son!"

Catlin stared at her with the blank face of a dreamer. Mrs Roberts took her by the shoulders and shook her hard. Then she repeated the order. This time Catlin nodded her head in mute agreement and went slowly out of the kitchen and out of the house.

Mrs Roberts, watching from her doorway, saw her gradually lengthen her stride until, when she was half-way across the field, she had bunched her skirts and was running as fast as she was able. Satisfied that help would soon be on its way, the mother turned back to her injured son.

When she reached Ty Garreg, Catlin did not waste time going into the house but ran straight to the stable yard where as usual, she found the lad Bryn. Out of breath as she was, and rather slow-witted as he was, it was a little time before she could make him understand what he had to do. But once he understood the urgency of the message he was quick to saddle Gracie and gallop off in search of Dr John Evans.

At last Catlin was free to sink down upon a bale of straw and rest. Free also to consider how best she could get into the house without her mother seeing her and bombarding her with questions regarding her bedraggled state. Briefly she wondered what had happened to Alun. There were no sounds from his old room above the stable where she would have expected him to go in the hope of escaping Hannah's vigilant eye. But, no doubt, she thought, he will have found a secure hiding place.

Here Catlin was mistaken. Alun had found no hiding place, nor indeed had he sought one. Instead, all bloody and muddied as he was, he had entered the house boldly by the front door. Hearing him blundering about the hall Hannah had come to investigate. Her startled scream when she saw him brought Non running from the kitchen. The two women stood staring in astonishment at the young man. His breeches were covered in mud. The sleeve of his once elegant coat had been half torn from the shoulder and hung down raggedly. The mud on his face mingled with the blood oozing from his cut and swollen lips. He stood swaying from side to side, his eyes bloodshot with rage.

"Do you see this, woman?" he cried. "Do you see this...?"

Surprisingly, it was young Non who first recovered her wits. She gently took Alun by the hand and told him firmly that he must come and sit down. Suddenly docile, Alun went with her as meekly as a child into the big slate floored kitchen with its high backed settle and the long scrubbed table where he had first sat and flirted with Nest and Non on that summer afternoon which now seemed so long ago.

By now Nest and Ianto had arrived on the scene and together they soon bathed and tended to Alun's wounds which were not after all so very serious. When they had finished, Ianto made to take him upstairs to his own room but Hannah who had stood silently by all this time, suddenly came to life. "No, no," she said, "take him out to the stable room, he is not fit for the house."

Slightly shocked by this unfeeling attitude, Ianto did as he was told. With Alun's arm resting on his shoulders, he led him slowly across the yard with Hannah following after. As they entered the shadowy old wooden building, Hannah was astonished to see Catlin half-sitting, half-lying on some bales of straw. The girl was in almost as great a state of disarray as Alun had been before Nest and Non had cleaned him up.

"Dear God," gasped Hannah, "What has happened to you?" Catlin was too exhausted to think of a reasonable answer so kept silent. Hannah then turned her attention to Alun, demanding, "What do you know of this? Tell me! Tell me, at once!" For a moment Alun hesitated. He looked from Catlin's pale face to Hannah's suspicious one and what he saw frightened him. Taking a sudden decision, he thrust Ianto aside and said to Hannah,

"I must talk to you alone concerning this. But first see to your daughter."

Seeing the sense of this and that he was not to be moved, Hannah took Catlin back to the house. There she removed her wet, muddy clothes and bathed her hands and face. Catlin all the time did not utter a word. Hannah soon found, to her relief, that the bloodstains on her daughter's hands and cloak did not spring from her own injuries. Feeling almost faint with relief, she helped the girl to bed and watched beside her until she fell into a deep sleep. Only then did she return to the stable to question Alun.

Alun had now had time to consider what was the best line of action for him to take. Whatever explanations he could give Hannah, however, must depend upon what Catlin had already told her. So he first asked how the girl was, and secondly, whether she had been able to give any account of their misfortunes.

"She has told me nothing," replied Hannah shortly, "And she is in no condition for me to question her. But I see you are somewhat recovered, so it is from you I shall expect to hear a true account."

Alun stifled a sigh of relief. So he still had time to make his departure before Catlin's tales brought Hannah's rage, of which he had a curious fear, bursting over him. He now launched into his partly-prepared story. As always with him, during the course of giving a fictional account of events, he succeeded to some extent in persuading himself of the truth of his own words. Indignantly and bitterly he accused Hannah...

"Have I not often warned you, told you that this is no place for us? Daily I have seen the suspicion, hatred, envy growing up around us. In my village it would have been so different. I could have been respected as a man of property, of family. But you would not let go of this place. You could not bear to give up your position as the Lady of Ty Garreg. What did you care for your good name or mine as long as you could rule over these damn muddy fields? What did you care that my heart was breaking for a new, clean life?"

Rage in another had always had the effect on Hannah of reducing her to an icy impassiveness. So now she waited quietly until Alun's blusterings had died away. Then she questioned him closely and calmly. "Do you mean to say that you and Catlin were set upon by infuriated neighbours on account of our secret relationship?"

"Secret?" cried Alun derisively, "Even the little bird scarers tell the crows about it!"

"But why Catlin?" persisted Hannah, "what has she done to so enrage folk that they should set upon her in this savage way?"

"Done?" said Alun bitterly, "she has done nothing except be your daughter, which is enough to make her accursed in their eyes. I tell you that if you stay here much longer you will have the place burnt about your ears, for the whole countryside is turning against you!"

For the first time, Hannah felt a slight shiver of fear quiver along her nerves but she kept her face impassive as she continued to question Alun about his recent experience, in particular how Catlin had come to be involved with him. And as Alun continued to lie, the more convincingly as the imagined picture he drew of two innocents being attacked by vicious peasants became more real to him. At last Hannah was convinced of the truth of his statement, that local feeling against her and her family because of her affair with her former farm labourer was reaching dangerous levels.

She left him and returned to the house. She went first to Catlin's room. The girl, startled out of sleep by her entrance, cried out in panic. Hastily Hannah sought to reassure her, settling her back upon the pillows and speaking softly to her.

She said, "Alun Ifans has told me how all this came about. You are safe now. Rest and I will see that such a terrible thing never happens again." Catlin stared at her mother in amazement. Why was Hannah so calm? How strange it all was, like a dream. Here exhaustion overtook her once more and she slipped back into an uneasy sleep. Hannah sat by her bedside for a long time. How bitterly she now regretted her involvement with Alun, the foolish infatuation that had brought this sorrow upon her beloved child. In that lonely vigil, any love she had still possessed for the sailor died away. She looked at him squarely recognising his good qualities, but also the fatal flaws, of greed, weakness, and insincerity. And she acknowledged that she must accept some responsibility for encouraging these traits to develop in him. She also acknowledged the fact that she could not, in her present vulnerable state, do without him.

The next morning Hannah summoned Alun to the parlour. His face was pale and bruised, but otherwise he seemed well enough. She asked him once again if he could identify any of his assailants. He answered as before, that he had seen them in the neighbourhood but he knew neither where they lived nor their names.

He watched Hannah uneasily as she sat thoughtfully staring down at her fingers as they tapped slowly on the desk. What was she thinking about! Suddenly she raised her head and looked directly into his eyes.

"This plan of yours for a boat. Are you sure that you can make it work, that you can govern it so as to provide a living for us all?"

Relieved that she had evidently accepted his account of the circumstances surrounding the fight of the day before, Alun launched into an enthusiastic explanation of how well he could provide for her were he only to be given a suitable vessel.

"There would be no need for long, expensive voyages" he told her. "Demand for the carrying of passengers and cargo to

Bristol and Liverpool grows daily. Only help me now, Hannah, and I will keep you like a lady for ever."

"Then I will get you the money," Hannah told him. "Only bear in mind that it is done at great cost to me; in more then money!"

"If it can be done," urged Alun, "then for God's sake do it. For we can no longer, in safety, stay here!"

"You may be right," agreed Hannah, "for there is a savagery in these country folk that once roused puts them beyond all reason. I think it best that you leave immediately and I will follow with the children as soon as I can arrange finances."

Alun hesitated, "I have very little money. Where shall I go? What shall I do?"

"I have been thinking about that," said Hannah. "You will need somewhere to stay while you are making enquiries about ships and cargoes. You will also need advice, for you are not a businessman. There is a miller living near Castell Coed who I believe comes from your part of the country. Evan Rees once described him to me as an honest fellow and a shrewd businessman. No doubt, for payment and perhaps for neighbourliness, he could be persuaded into providing you with a lodging and might very well provide you with advice into the bargain. As for money for your immediate needs - I have more than enough for that." So saying, she took from her desk drawer the two neat packets she had made of all the coins and notes she had by her and gave them to him.

Alun tried to conceal his eagerness as he took the packets, which had a most pleasantly weighty feel about them. He also struggled to conceal the tide of jubilation at the thought of freedom, which, filling his chest and rising to his throat, threatened to choke him with its intensity.

Hannah accepted his silence and strange looks as springing from his fear at the thought of leaving the shelter of Ty Garreg and taking on new heavy responsibilities. She briskly took charge of his preparations for departure. Such few clothes as she judged necessary were soon packed into a neat roll. With this on his back, together with a small packet of food to last him the journey, Alun was ready to leave. He quickly made such farewells as he thought necessary, giving market business as a reason for his journey. To his relief he was spared from having to say good-bye to Catlin since she was still asleep. Hannah herself took him to the great front door. He heard the familiar grate as it was pulled back over the worn step, they clasped hands briefly and then he was gone.

When he reached the road that ran along the hill above Ty Garreg, he turned to look back at the house. It stood there on its own small plateau, silhouetted against the distant hills. The morning sky which had started bright had now darkened. The clouds now hanging low and threatening over the landscape were tinged with a strange light as the partially obscured sun struck through their blackness. This light falling on Ty Garreg, turned its grey stones a cloudy green so that the house against its background of mist-laden hills and black clouds seemed to float, ghost-like, insubstantial as a dream. Qualities it shared with its inhabitants, or so it now seemed to him.

He tried to picture them as they must be now, working about the house at their usual daily tasks. He could see them plainly enough in his mind's eye but they appeared as if he were recalling scenes from long ago. They had nothing to do with the reality of him standing there in a good pair of boots, with money in his pocket and a storm coming up. He adjusted his pack more comfortably on his shoulders and restarted his journey. The sky became every minute more threatening and he was eager to reach shelter of some kind before the rains came. At the junction of two roads he paused for a moment as he looked to where the broader road continued on to Newbridge and beyond that to the high road that led out of Wales into England. Then, still obedient to Hannah's will, he turned into the narrower way which led down into the wide valley which encircled Castell Coed.

CHAPTER XXII

Once more Hannah sat at her desk going through her business affairs in wearisome detail. Once again she reached the same conclusion, that her only way out of her difficulties was either to sell or mortgage Ty Garreg. No word had come to her from Gomer Morgan and she now felt certain that he meant to do nothing to help her break the entail. There remained one trump card she could play which would force his hand but this she was reluctant to use. She valued her brother-in-law's good opinion of her and did not, even now, want to admit the inevitability of losing it. She now justified to herself the postponement of a visit to his office by the necessity she felt there was to care for Catlin.

For two days the girl lay in bed, refusing food, shielding her eyes from the light. At first Hannah treated her with tender care but as time passed and her anxieties rose, so did her temper. On the third morning it snapped. Brusquely she ordered her daughter to get up, go downstairs and eat her porridge. That having been done, she was to accompany the rest of the family to church.

Tearfully protesting, Catlin nevertheless did as she was told. Despite her initial reluctance to attempt the hearty breakfast Nest had prepared for her, she found to her surprise that as she ate, her appetite grew. Rarely had food tasted so good. She sat savouring the warmth and familiar atmosphere of the kitchen. She had dreaded meeting Alun again and it was with relief that she heard of his departure. She could not help wondering at herself. Perhaps, she thought, grief will come later.

The Morgans were the cynosure of all eyes as they walked through the churchyard to the little ancient church. No one knew exactly what had happened that day when Dr John Evans had had to be summoned so dramatically to tend the schoolmaster. Nor why that upstart farm bailiff from Ty Garreg had left the district the very next day. But this lack of definite knowledge only lent spice to their speculation and intensity to their interest. However, these earnest seekers after truth got little response either to open stares or sidelong glances. Thomas and Owen went happily along, jostling and joking with each other as usual. Catlin walked quietly and decorously, entirely enwrapped in her own thoughts. And Hannah, she treated all she met with such a wide blank stare that some weaker souls were almost driven to pinching themselves to make sure that after all they were really there.

It was a raw, damp morning and the air inside the church was hardly warmer than that outside. The old slate floor had absorbed so much moisture that it gleamed blackly wet as though newly washed and not yet dried. Everywhere, including the pews, was cold and clammy to the touch. At the entry of the Morgans a soft, rustling sigh disturbed the usual pre-service solemnity as all heads turned to watch them.

Sarah Morris, the vicar's widowed daughter, was one of those who looked across at the Morgan pew. Like everyone else she had heard something about the fight involving Catlin. Her gaze was drawn to Catlin's extreme pallor and her sympathetic heart prompted her to do what she next did. Ignoring her mother's outraged glare she left her pew to cross to the Morgans'. After greeting Hannah she turned to Catlin and taking the girl's hands in hers spoke softly.

"Miss Morgan, I fear you have been ill and are not yet quite recovered. I must ask you to pardon my remissness in not calling upon you sooner but my duties have kept me at home a good deal. May I have your permission, and that of your mother, to call upon you within the next few days?"

Startled out of her reverie, Catlin looked into the kind, rather plain face. What she saw there reassured and touched her heart so that she cried out impulsively,

"Oh yes, please do and very soon, for you know..." and here her voice faltered, "I am often very lonely."

"Are we not all, from time to time?" answered Sarah quietly, and after arranging to call the next day she returned to her seat, only now becoming aware of her father's fury as his daughter's 'antics' held up the proper progress of the service.

The next day, Sarah, true to her words, called at Ty Garreg. Strangely enough she had never been there before. She had been quite grown up when her father took up his parish duties there and she had married shortly afterwards. There had never been much visiting between the vicarage and Ty Garreg. Hannah regarded the cleric as a fat, lazy priest and suspected his wife of spiteful gossip. The Morgans, being the biggest landowners in the district, the Reverend Williams had thought it politic to keep in with them and the civilities had been observed; although his resentment at the necessity of having to do so had greatly increased since Thomas Morgan's death had left Hannah in charge.

Sarah had brought her little boy with her and the child helped to bridge the first few awkward moments as both sides tried to forget that neither family had thought much of each other in the past. They did this so successfully that within a short time Hannah found that she was regretting her neglect of the entire Williams family simply because of her dislike of the father. She found Sarah to be as mannerly and pleasant a visitor as she could have wished and was pleased to see the effect of company upon Catlin's low spirits. When old Nest lured the pretty boy away to the kitchen with promises of 'sugary cakes', the two girls (for Sarah was only a few years older than Catlin) were free to go off to Catlin's room. There they passed a happy hour in light-hearted chatter, discovering to their delight the many tastes they had in common.

That night as Catlin lay in bed, she forgot to weep for Alun. Instead, she went over in her mind the pleasant afternoon. As she remembered how Sarah had curled up on the foot of her bed, hands clasped around her knees, she was reminded of similar afternoons spent with Lettis at Castell Coed. How much she had enjoyed those frivolous hours and how pleased she had been to have Lettis as a friend. But Sarah was so superior to Lettis, her mind so much more akin to her own, so altogether more to her liking and moreover she lived so very near; they could see each other every day. 'At last,' said Catlin to herself, 'At last I have a real friend.'

In her happiness Catlin even found time to think of Hannah. 'How badly I have treated her lately,' she thought. 'How ungrateful I have been for the fact that she has never once reproached me for my deceit and impropriety!' For Catlin was still unaware that Hannah did not know that she had been the cause of the fight between Aeros and Alun. 'Oh I will be so much more loving, I will be so very good to her,' thought Catlin and, so thinking, fell asleep.

Sarah Morris did indeed become a frequent visitor to the house. Catlin took great pleasure in her company, liking her more each time they met. Her improved spirits made for more contentment in the house. The placid atmosphere and her happier relationship with Catlin had a curious effect upon Hannah. Instead of binding her closer to Ty Garreg they gave her the courage to contemplate leaving its shelter and going out in search of a wider future. She sent Bryn into Newbridge with a message for Gomer saying that she would call upon him in three days time to discuss a most serious matter. On receiving this missive, Gomer felt a deep sense of foreboding. It was evident that his favourite prophylaxis against trouble (which was to do nothing) had not been effective this time. He prepared himself for a very difficult interview.

No amount of preparation, however, would have served to steel Gomer against the knowledge of the truly dreadful facts which Hannah now laid before him. He found it almost unbelievable that the seemingly secure structure of life at Ty Garreg should have reached this point of collapse in the less than eighteen months that had passed since his brother's death.

Could it really be true that the family was in danger of being driven from the neighbourhood? He had heard of humbler folk being driven from their squalid homes by gangs of roistering youths who had taken upon themselves the responsibility for public morality as they saw it. But surely this could not happen to such eminently respectable people of good standing as the Morgans. Again Hannah assured him that indeed it could and looking at her pale and desperate face, Gomer was driven to believe she must be right.

However, he had to warn her again, that however great the necessity, there was no way in which there could be a public sale of Ty Garreg.

"I have thought long and hard about this problem," he said. "The only solution I can find is that I take over the guardianship of the estate. For that to be possible you would have to be declared unfit to carry out any longer the various duties connected with its management." Here he allowed himself a touch of grim humour. "A weakness of the mind would probably be the most effective plea. As to the costs, I already have your estimate of the amount you would require to set you up elsewhere. It is less than the property would fetch on the open market but I cannot help that. I am not a wealthy man and besides, the children's expenses will continue to grow."

Hannah's eyes opened wide with shock, as did her mouth. "But the children will be with me. You cannot think I meant otherwise?"

For the first time Gomer's face expressed the anger that up until now he had successfully concealed.

"Do you suppose," he told her, "that I have so little regard for my dead brother's memory that I would allow his innocent children to live with an immoral woman and her paramour, even if she is their mother? Take the money and go. If you have any sense of decency left, or any true love for your children, you will never return to blight their young lives further."

In vain, Hannah argued, ranted, even wept. Gomer remained adamant. If he gave her the money, she must go and leave the children with him. He even hinted that he believed he already had enough legal grounds to permit him to assume their guardianship whether she agreed to it or not. In which case, he reminded her, there would be no question of the transfer of large sums of money. A small payment only might be made, to save her from actual starvation.

At last, Hannah had to admit defeat. A take-over date of four weeks hence was agreed upon. A large deposit was paid over to Hannah immediately, the balance would be remitted on the day she left Ty Garreg.

It was a pale and shaken woman whom Gomer escorted to the door. Touched by a moment of compunction, he asked her if she would like him to drive her home. Hannah brushed his offer aside impatiently; she had no wish to spend any more time in the company of this unsympathetic stranger, which was what Gomer had become to her. Actually relieved to be out of her company, Gomer closed the door thankfully behind her. Now he must find Gwladys and tell her of the great change that was to come about in their lives. He had some misgivings as to how she would view certain aspects of the move. He had never noticed that she had any particular affection for the two lively little boys, nor had she any great liking for Catlin. Unquestionably, there would be difficulties. But he believed that her pleasure at becoming the mistress of Ty Garreg would, for her, outweigh any disadvantages.

CHAPTER XXIII

Catlin was soon called upon to put into practice her resolution to 'be good to Hannah'. At the sound of wheels below her window Catlin had hastened downstairs and out to meet her mother, expecting that she would need help with the often exciting pile of packages that she usually brought back from town. But this time there were no parcels to be carried in, only her mother as she had never seen her before: pale, trembling and in a state of near collapse.

As quickly as she could, Catlin helped her into the house, but when she would have turned into the parlour, Hannah stopped her and indicated that she wanted to go to her room. With her daughter's help she was soon undressed and lying in her bed. Catlin was almost overcome with panic as she looked down at her mother's face. All colour had drained from it except for the purple smudges under the dark eyes that stared at Catlin as if she hardly knew her. 'I must get her a doctor, food and drink,' she thought confusedly but as she reached the door Hannah cried out her name. Until now she had not spoken a word. When Catlin ran back to the bed, Hannah threw her arms around her and burst into hysterical sobbing. She would not answer Catlin's frantic questions but simply repeated her name over and over again.

Eventually Hannah's hysterics were calmed and with the help of a soothing drink concocted by Nest, she fell into an exhausted sleep. Only then did Catlin go to her own room where she sat for a long time, feeling sorely troubled.

Hannah woke early the next morning and lay quietly in the dark, watching the square of window lighten. She had only muddled memories of the day before and these she soon dismissed from her mind. The time for weeping was over. She was completely calm now as she reviewed the situation. Odious as Gomer's conditions were to her, she could see no alternative to accepting them. 'At least for the time being,' she thought.

Already her natural optimism was returning. Gomer's threats of legal action against her had thoroughly frightened her at the time but now she did not fully believe in their validity. Staring into the shadows, she considered and then dismissed the idea of life without Catlin. The girl would soon be of age and in any case she could not see her consenting to live with Gwladys for long. The boys, being younger, were more of a problem. She visualised them, their sturdy fairness, their abounding energy, their often too loud voices. Frankly, she had never been greatly attached to them. Indeed, for a while she had seen them primarily as rivals - here her mind shied nervously away from the memory of a package bobbing along on a slow tide - but whatever her feelings or lack of them, she could not accept the idea of Gwladys being in possession of her sons, her children. For the time being, she conceded she had no option; she must leave them behind. However, once she and Alun were married, established in business, in possession of money, then surely there would be much that could be done.

Having settled these questions in her mind, she rose, dressed and went downstairs. There she surprised everyone with her calm, matter of fact manner. Within a short time it was as if the events following her arrival home the previous day had never happened. The boys were sent cheerfully off to school, Catlin reminded of an engagement she had with Sarah Morris, Nest and Non set about their usual work and Hannah herself retired to the parlour after asking that Bryn be sent to her.

While waiting for the boy to appear, Hannah swiftly wrote a short letter to Alun. She told him of the arrangement she had made with Gomer that in return for a good sum of money he should take over Ty Garreg. She said she would be ready to leave the farm in four weeks' time, or earlier if he could provide her with somewhere to go. She urged him to make plans for their future lives together as soon as possible. To make this easier for him she enclosed most of the money she had received from Gomer as a down-payment on Ty Garreg.

When Bryn arrived she gave him careful directions as to how to find the mill where she thought it most likely Alun would be staying. If he was not there, she told the boy, he must find out where he had gone. The miller would most likely be able to help him. Whatever difficulties there were, she emphasised he must find Alun Ifans and deliver the packet into his hands and his alone.

Flattered at the trust imposed in him and excited at the prospect of what he saw as a positive adventure, for he had never travelled so far on his own before, Bryn soon made himself ready to leave. When he had gone, Hannah cast her mind about as to what other preparations she could be making. She resolved to start sorting out those household items she regarded as being particularly her own, either because she had brought them with her as a bride, or she had bought them since, or simply because she particularly liked them. She decided to start with the linen cupboard, fine linen being a great passion of hers. It was there that Catlin found her when she returned home from her visit to Sarah.

Hastening along the corridor to her room to remove her outdoor garments, Catlin was surprised to find her way blocked by a positive mountain of household linen to which Hannah was constantly adding as she dragged item after item from the depth of the capacious cupboard.

"Why are you doing this now?" asked Catlin, "it is hardly springtime."

"It is a task long overdue," answered Hannah. "I really do believe that some of this stuff has not seen the light of day since before you were born. Quickly, get your bonnet off and come and help me or I shall not be done by dinnertime!"

They were soon working happily side by side, sorting out the linen into its various categories of use and value. Suddenly Hannah laughed.

"Do you remember how I caught you trying to carry off my best embroidered linen sheets to cut up for pinafores?"

"Indeed I do," said Catlin, "what a happy day that was!"

Hannah caught a wistful note in her daughter's voice and looked at her keenly.

"Why do you never go down to the school now?" she asked. "Did the schoolmaster frighten you off with a proposal?"

"Of course not, Mother," Catlin protested, "he has never said anything of the kind to me!"

"Well, he may have done," replied Hannah, "if I had not let him and his scheming mother know that such an offer would be most unwelcome!"

"Oh mother, what have you done?" whispered Catlin, "why did you not tell me of this?"

"Because at the time I thought it best not to. They have no money, no position. I hoped for a better match for you than that. But now," she added bleakly "who knows, you may be glad of the support of such a one as Aeros Roberts!"

"Indeed, I would be," snapped Catlin, "For he is a good and kind man." But she looked at Hannah keenly, "Why should you think so now and not then? What is going to happen to us? Why were you so distressed yesterday on your return from Newbridge?"

Hannah felt a sudden impulse to confide in her daughter. How pleasant it would be to share both her present problems and her fears for the future with her. But as she looked across the piles of linen at the girl's concerned face, she knew that it was impossible. For the simple reason that she could not find the words, the clear unshockable words to convey to her so much that would be shocking to her. At some time it must be done, but not now when they were so close and happy together. So she simply said, brusquely, that there was nothing wrong, and that there had been too much talking and not enough working.

But Catlin persisted, "I know there is. For a long time now there has been a strangeness in the house. It was not just because father died. Oh, we were all terribly sad and we missed him terribly, but other things stayed the same. But now everything has changed. I think I noticed it first when I came back from Castell Coed the second time. Sometimes I think you do not love us, the boys and I, any longer. Why should it be so? What have we done?"

"Oh, my dearest girl," sighed Hannah, "you have done nothing wrong, and you are right, there has been much that is wrong in this house of late. I cannot explain it to you now but I promise you will know everything soon. When you do, promise me that you will remember that I love you, and do believe that, if it is possible, I will one day make all things right again."

With this promise, Catlin had to be content, although it hardly served to comfort her. Together they quickly finished sorting the linen and returned it to the shelves, except, that was, for the very best sheets and pillowcases which together with the damask tablecloths were parcelled up and carried off to Hannah's room. Catlin forbore to comment on this, however, as she felt she had questioned enough for one morning.

Over the next few days, Hannah continued to carry away some of the best household items and fine ornaments to her room which soon began to resemble a veritable Aladdin's cave. Catlin became increasingly disturbed at this strange behaviour and wished very much she had someone she could discuss it with. She felt close enough to Sarah by now to confide in her but she was afraid that she in her turn might confide in her own mother. She knew how very angry Hannah would be if she should ever find out that Mrs Williams had been told any secrets about her. There was Evan Rees but he lived so far away and besides this, Catlin had an uneasy feeling that he had passed out of their lives for good. She was partly sad about this, and partly glad since it meant they would not have to leave Ty Garreg.

To speak to her uncle Gomer would be to risk meeting her aunt Gwladys and that she did not want to do ever again, if that could possibly be arranged! No, there really was no one, unless - a sudden thought came to her. Why should she not consult Aeros? Perhaps it was true what her mother had said, perhaps he did love her. He would, therefore, be all the more ready to help her. Then she remembered, with a blush of shame, the circumstances of their last meeting. But she also remembered how she had helped him home and once there, how he had shielded her from his mother's curiosity. Surely he could not think so badly of her if he had done that. Resolutely stifling all her misgivings, she ran to get her cloak and bonnet and was soon crossing the quiet fields to Ysgol Maesbach.

The children had gone home and Aeros was busily setting the classroom to rights. Hearing a step at the door, he looked up and to his amazement saw Catlin standing there. They had not met since his fight with Alun Ifans and he had gloomily supposed that she would never speak to him again. Now he stammered as he greeted her,

"Why, Miss Morgan."

Catlin forgot her initial embarrassment in her amusement at being so formally addressed.

"Miss Morgan!" she laughed, "I really must have grown very grand these days, that you forget to call me Catlin!" Now they were both laughing and in doing so regained their old easy relationship. A few dusty ashes still glowed in the bottom of the stove and Aeros, recklessly piling on some of his precious fuel, soon coaxed it into a blaze. Two chairs were drawn up and for a few minutes they sat in companionable silence.

Then Aeros spoke, hesitantly at first, "I have not seen you since that dreadful day. I have often wondered if you would ever come here again."

Catlin coloured but lifted her head and met his eyes resolutely, "I did not come here because I was ashamed to meet you!"

"You had no need to be," said Aeros, "I have thought since that perhaps what I did that day was wrong. That maybe I should not have interfered. Please believe I only did so because I cared for you!"

"I do believe that," said Catlin and for a while they sat in silence again. Then Catlin said, "I came here today because I very much need someone to talk to. Someone who can give me good advice. I need a friend!"

"You know I will always be that," Aeros assured her. "So tell me what is wrong and I will help if I can!"

"It is about my mother," began Catlin.

"Did she find out? Is she terribly angry with you?" interjected Aeros.

"No, no," answered Catlin, "that is to say, yes, she knew everything from that very day and she forgave me and told me not to worry. She has never mentioned the matter to me since and she has never reproached me. Really she has been like an angel to me."

Aeros listened to this statement with some scepticism. He had never regarded Hannah as a likely candidate for sainthood.

And in circumstances like these, where a daughter had not only endangered her own reputation but stolen her mother's lover into the bargain! Well, even the most reasonable mother might be forgiven a certain irascibility! Yet Catlin seemed quite certain that Hannah did not hold any grudge against her.

He wondered if she knew of her mother's relationship with Alun Ifans and in order to find out, ventured a tentative question.

"How does your mother regard Alun Ifans now?" he asked her.

"I think we will never see him again," answered Catlin.

This was hardly conclusive but Aeros felt he could pursue the matter no further at this state. He turned to another subject. "There was talk of a match between your mother and Evan Rees of Castell Coed. Is that still to take place?"

"I think not," said Catlin, "for he never writes or visits. My mother never mentions him these days and once when I asked her about him she grew very angry!" Aeros nodded. This at least fitted in with the gossip he had heard about Hannah.

"You have not yet told me," he said gently, "What it is that is worrying you so much."

Then Catlin told him of her mother's strange moods, of the servants' silence, of the general air of unease in the house. Aeros heard all this with much misgiving. What was Hannah planning? Had Alun Ifans really gone? He had heard a rumour that he had been seen in several public houses in the area, boasting that he had plenty of money in his pocket. If he came back or Hannah went to join him how would this affect the children? His first concern was for Catlin but he also felt protective towards the two little boys who were his pupils. He determined to find out all he could about Hannah's activities during the next few days. In the meantime he attempted to reassure Catlin that most of her worries were unnecessary.

Looking up at the high windows, he was surprised to see how dark it had become. "I must take you home quickly," he said, "they will be sending out a search party for you!" He went into the schoolhouse to fetch a coat and a lantern and then arm in arm they set off across the fields. It was a very dark night with a young moon giving only a glimmer of light but the stars shone brilliant and huge against the black sky and the lantern spilled a little pool of gold around their feet. The peace of that walk with the warmth of Aeros's arm in hers and the little circle of light from the lantern shielding them from the black darkness all around, did much to erase from Catlin's mind the horrific memory of their last stumbling journey through the fields. When they reached Ty Garreg, Aeros refused to come in but he stood watching by the gate until he was sure that she was safely inside the house.

Catlin ran quickly down the hall and was halfway up the stairs before she noticed a light in the parlour. Slowly she retraced her steps and opened the door. Hannah was sitting on the floor surrounded by all the silverware that Catlin had known, and some she had not known, they possessed. Hannah looked up absently,

"Where have you been?" she asked and without waiting for a reply, she continued, "get cloths and polishes and come to help, for all this must be cleaned."

"It is dinnertime, mother," Catlin reminded her gently.

"Then we shall do it later," announced Hannah firmly and continued to compare the merits of two different sets of teaspoons.

CHAPTER XXIV

The next day, Aeros questioned Thomas and Owen as discreetly as he could. It soon became obvious that the two boys knew nothing of any plans to leave Ty Garreg. The only piece of information they gave Aeros that was of any interest to him was that Bryn had told them that Alun Ifans, whom they much admired, was living the life of a fine gentleman and that he was soon to be married. 'Married,' mused Aeros. 'But to whom?'

Disappointed in the boys as sources of information, Aeros turned to his mother. Despite her life of semi-seclusion Mrs Roberts had the knack of gathering up all the available gossip of the neighbourhood. However, she was sulking because Catlin had not seen fit to call in on her on her last visit, and because her son had refused to discuss it with her. Now she would only issue dark and vague warnings as to the advisability of keeping away from the family at Ty Garreg. Somewhat exasperated, Aeros abandoned his detective work for the time being, but determined to keep his ears and eyes open for any further developments that might concern Catlin. He also made a point of walking each evening to a point where he could look down upon the house and satisfy himself that it was still in occupation.

Meanwhile, Catlin was becoming more and more distressed by her mother's behaviour. At times Hannah would be most affectionate and loving, at others, coldly distant. But whatever her mood, she continued her magpie activities. While in work or conversation, she would suddenly fix her eyes on some object and, if it pleased her, she would quickly carry it off to her room.

Catlin feared that all this stress was affecting her mother's health and indeed, there were some mornings when Hannah looked deathly pale and could scarcely rise from her bed. But all Catlin's remonstrances had no effect on her and she continued in her strange ways.

Hannah herself, was quite oblivious to the fact that her behaviour was exciting comment. In her own opinion she was being eminently rational in trying to rescue what she could from what she regarded as the approaching sack of Ty Garreg.

Two weeks had passed since her visit to Gomer and she began to look impatiently for a letter from Alun. When none came, she sent Bryn once again to the mill. This time he came back with the news that Alun Ifans was not there. The miller had told him that he was away buying a boat. Hannah frowned at this. Had not the plan been to buy a vessel large enough to carry cargoes and passengers? But perhaps, she cheered herself, Bryn had misunderstood. A boat, a ship, all were the same to these land working peasants. No doubt Alun was arranging to pay a deposit on a small coastal craft and would soon be writing to her regarding this.

But still no letter came. Hannah began to stare at the calendar as if mesmerised. Almost within days they would be at the point fixed for Gomer's entry into Ty Garreg. She still had said nothing of this to Catlin or anyone else in the house. She had also another worry. She did not know how much longer she could conceal her condition. Already she was finding it difficult to lace her corset and she fancied that Nest's eyes were resting speculatively on her.

One morning she rose early in a fine flurry of activity. She went to the yard and roused Bryn from his pallet bed to harness the gig for her. Then, without waiting for breakfast, she took the road to Castell Coed. Deep in thought, she hardly noticed the miles slip by. At last she reached the outskirts of the little town and within a few minutes was in the High Street. She drove past Evan's house without a glance, then up the hill and was soon out in the country again. Another mile and then there was the little hunched mill, buried deep in its grove of straggling trees.

At the sound of the gig the miller himself came to the door. He looked with some dismay at Hannah's pale, set face and went back into the house to call his daughter. When the girl came out and saw Hannah, she muttered an oath to herself but took the reins civilly enough and steadied the horse while Hannah dismounted.

Hannah told the girl that she wanted to speak to her father and the girl rather sullenly led her into the house. Once again Hannah found herself in the small, dark room with the thick glassed window overlooking the falls. When the miller came she noticed how he avoided her eyes as she questioned him as to the whereabouts of Alun Ifans. The man blusteringly denied at first that he had ever been at the mill. Outraged at this blatant falsehood Hannah told him that she had a witness who would swear that he had seen the sailor at the mill. She went on to threaten the miller. She told him that she had influential friends in the neighbourhood who would ensure that his business was ruined if he continued to tell her falsehoods. At this the miller grew aggressive. 'What cared he for her fine friends?' he said. As to the business he had already sold it. He had no need for such a penny-pinching occupation now that his daughter was making a good match and he was going into partnership with his future son-in-law.

Hannah looked at him in some bewilderment. What had his lumpish daughter's matrimonial plans to do with this present situation? Why was this idiot denying that Alun had ever been there? She had a sudden chilling thought. 'Surely he could not have done away with him for the sake of the money?' She had heard of such things. Suddenly she felt weak and sick and afraid of being alone in the house with this unprepossessing couple. She had a sudden urge to escape. She turned to leave and in doing so caught her foot in a rug. She fell heavily, bruising her side against a heavy table. She felt a deep stab of pain and the room spun round her. Then the girl's strong arms were round her and she was being helped to her feet and into a chair.

As the room stopped spinning and her head began to clear, she gasped out a request for water. When it arrived, her hands were shaking too much for her to hold the glass so it was the girl who held it to her lips. She took a few gulps and then made to push the glass away. As she did so, her eyes fell on the large freckled hand that held the glass. On the fourth finger, for it was not big enough to go on any other, gleamed a garnet ring in an intricate setting of twisted gold wires.

Hannah sat up straight and spoke in cold composed tones. "Where did you get that ring?" she asked.

"What's that to you?" answered the girl rudely.

"I believe it to be mine." answered Hannah.

"How can it be yours," blustered the girl, "when it is on my hand?"

"It is mine!" said Hannah. "And I think you must have stolen it. If you do not return it to me immediately and tell me how you obtained it, I shall inform the police."

The miller come alive at this threat and raising his voice in anger, shouted, "How dare you accuse honest folk of thievery. Tell her, Modlen, tell her that the ring was given to you by your sweetheart."

"Her sweetheart," gasped Hannah, "and who is he?"

"Why 'tis Alun Ifans, as I believe you know, Missus. A lad I knew long ago and fancied lost at sea. Then one morning, he comes here, out of the blue, and tells a most strange tale of how a wealthy widow had lured him away from his first true love, my daughter here. But that now he had come to his senses and wanted nothing more to do with her; especially now that he had found Modlen again. And you should take notice of this, Missus, and go back peacefully to your own place. For we are all going back to where we belong and will trouble no-one any more."

While still not understanding how the ring had come into Alun's possession, Hannah recognised the futility of questioning them further. Nor had she any wish to repossess the ring. She could never have seen it again without also seeing the coarse hand it now adorned. Wearily she got up and walked out of the house to where her gig was standing. In silence the girl helped her climb into the seat and then placed the reins in her hands. Looking up into her face she said with rough kindliness, "He was no sort of man for you, lady. You are better off without him." Hannah looked down at her, noting how alike she was, despite her plainness, to the handsome Alun.

"He will rob and cheat you as he has done me," she said to the girl.

"Not I, Missus," she answered. "We are two of a kind, he'd never get the better of me!"

As Hannah drove the long lonely way home to Ty Garreg, she went over and over in her mind the question as to how Alun came into possession of the Morgan family ring. Could he have stolen it? She doubted it. Although he had robbed and deceived her on a grand scale, she did not think petty thievery was part of his nature. For the moment, the larger problems that now overhung her future were eclipsed as her mind, perhaps in self-defence, occupied itself exclusively with the question of the ring.

On reaching home, she went at once in search of Catlin. She found her in her room rearranging the small collection of shells and pieces of quartz that she kept as ornaments on her windowsills. Hannah stood watching her unobserved for a moment and then, almost to her own surprise, she said quietly, "Catlin, why did you give the garnet ring to Alun Ifans?"

Any doubts she may have had as to the rightness of her conjecture were dispelled by the expression of frightened guilt on her daughter's face. The giving away of the garnet ring, the heirloom ring, was the one fact which Catlin had been most eager to conceal from Hannah, who now repeated her question.

At last Catlin found the courage to say, "It was a love token, given in exchange for his own ring." She went quickly to her dressing table and took out the silver ring which Alun had given her that day on the beach when he had told her he was leaving. She put the ring into Hannah's hands, who stood looking down at it in complete mystification.

"A love token," she murmured, "what do you mean, Catlin?"

Now it was the turn of Catlin to be mystified.

"You know what I mean," she cried, "You know everything, you said so."

As Hannah sprang at her, seized her by the shoulders and shook her violently, "What do I know?" she screamed, "what do I know?"

Thoroughly frightened, Catlin screamed back what she thought Hannah had already known. When she had finished Hannah stared at her in horror.

"So it was you," she whispered. "All the time it was you who was taking him away from me. You fool, you little fool, you have ruined us all. All this time, were you plotting together, were you laughing at me, or were you really so simple that you knew nothing, meant nothing?"

"I don't understand," sobbed Catlin, "what was it to do with you? How have I hurt you?"

"You don't know, you really don't know?" said Hannah. "Then listen carefully while I tell you how it was." And she proceeded to tell Catlin how she had been infatuated with Alun Ifans, had become pregnant by him and was now completely ruined, having been forced to sign away home and children.

Catlin listened in a daze to what seemed to her an almost incredible story.

Her mind at last fastened on one simple fact. "How could you forget my father so soon?" she asked.

"Your father?" sneered Hannah, "and who was that, pray?"

"Why, it was Thomas Morgan, of course," said Catlin falteringly, as if she already knew the answer. But her voice grew stronger as she continued, "If he were alive today, you would not treat me so."

"Your father," hissed Hannah, "was a damned primping, posing dancing master, and it was because of him and of you that I was forced to leave the home I loved and come and live in this cursed backwater. But no," she added sarcastically, "I am being unfair. It was not because of you alone. It was also because of me. Because I was a harlot and a whore, as you have become after me. Like mother, like daughter!" She struck the girl across the face with brutal strength and then left the room.

All the rest of that long day, Catlin lay alone in her cold room. Hannah had given orders that no one should approach her. Little Owen did, in fact, creep to her door and scratch gently upon it, but receiving no answer, crept quietly away again.

As the day ended, a storm blew up. The winds whined in the chimneys, sending gusts of smoke billowing back into the rooms. Sheets of rain hurled themselves against the windows with such ferocity that it seemed that at any moment they would be smashed to pieces. Outside the house all was noise and action, inside all silent gloom. Even the boys played in whispers and the grown-ups sat in silence, oppressed by the knowledge of Catlin alone in her dark room.

At last it was time to light candles and lamps and carry them upstairs. Since the scene with Catlin, Hannah had not allowed herself to think or feel. The actions she performed were purely mechanical, requiring no deliberate thought. She went to her room, undressed, slid between icy sheets and fell asleep immediately.

Catlin waited until the house fell silent. Then she rose and moving quickly about her room, packed a small bag as best she could by the light of a single candle. She had no plans, no idea of where she might go. All she knew was that she must leave the house. That she could never face anyone there ever again.

As she crept down the stairs, every step seemed to scream a warning as the old wood shifted and creaked beneath her feet. She reached the hall and at last was standing by the front door. She tugged at the stiff bolts and at last succeeded in sending them crashing back. The noise they made seemed to echo endlessly through the house. She held her breath but no one stirred, no one came running or called her name. As she dragged the great door open she heard the familiar grating noise it made as it scraped back over the stone floor. Then she was out on the front steps with the icy winds tearing at her skirts and pulling her hair out of its pins.

Upstairs, Hannah suddenly awoke. She lay still for a while, wondering what had disturbed her sleep. She could hear nothing more unusual than the sounds of the storm as it raged around the house. Impulsively, she slid out of bed, and lighting her lamp, went out on to the landing. She leant over the banisters and stared down into the thick darkness. All was silent. She went into the boys' room. They were both sleeping soundly; each wrapped and cocooned in his own tangle of bedclothes. She then went to Catlin's room, listened outside the door and then pushed it open. Lifting her lamp high, she looked around the room, and saw it was empty. For a moment her heart jumped in panic, then the cold hatred she now felt for the girl steadied it. 'So she is gone,' she thought. 'Good riddance to evil rubbish.' She closed the door and returned to her own room.

Catlin was surprised by the wind. It was colder and stronger than she had expected. She half-turned to go back into the house, but the heavy door had swung to behind her. If she wanted to go back she would have to rouse the house and that she would not do.

She summoned up all her courage and plunged out into the blackness. Holding her breath she stumbled around the corner of the house and up into the field behind. The ground was wet and slippery with mud and the climb was hard. When she reached the narrow road that ran across the top of the field, she hesitated for a moment. She looked towards the left where the road led inland, but the winds were blowing fiercely from that direction and instinctively she went with them, down the hill towards the sea. She went quickly, half blown along between the leafless hedges. The path was littered with broken branches and small twigs which had been brought down by the storm. They cracked beneath her feet and more than once caused her to trip and fall.

As she went down, she passed several paths leading off the main track, but they all led upwards into the teeth of the wind. Buffeted by the gales, dazed by the constantly changing light as the moon was now revealed, now obscured by sheets of scudding clouds, she continued instinctively to choose the easiest path which alone seemed to promise a destination, a place of sanctuary.

As the path came to its deep end, the howl of the wind was joined by the crash of the waves. Quite suddenly it seemed the track broadened and there was the beach. Around the small cove the cliffs rose unendingly high and black but between them the beach stretched soft and white, as inviting as a feather bed. But when she stumbled thankfully down into it, she found the soft whiteness was nothing more than masses of whipped up foam which clung to her skirts and soaked through to her skin. Here was no sanctuary, no place of safety, only the end of the world. The only way out was by the path she had just come by and that led only to the place she had so desperately run from.

And down that path too, still roared the killing winds which had helped her to that place of ultimate loneliness.

She could not face the challenge of the menacing road, nor the cold embrace of the deceitful beach. The moon, appearing at that moment in a space between the clouds, revealed a narrow gully to her left which led down into a tangle of bushes. She turned tiredly down into it in the hope of finding a place where she could shelter from the flying foam and sand.

The farmer's dogs found her the next morning where she had fallen from the treacherous path. Their excited barking brought the farmer's son running to investigate. Back at the farm, the men brought out the old farm sledge which was so much better than a wheeled cart on the steep Welsh hills. They tied her on to it, lest she should slip again, and took her sadly home to Ty Garreg.

Hannah had stood all morning staring out of her parlour window. When she saw the little procession coming over the hill, it was as if she had expected it. Without haste she went out of the door and down the steps. She stood there and waited until the sledge stopped at her feet. Then she told the men in a completely emotionless voice to take the girl to her room.

Overawed as much by her strange manner as by the tragedy, the men did as they were told in silence. When they had gone she locked the door and approached the bed.

Catlin's face was streaked with mud, her hair straggled over her shoulders in lank, seaweed-like strands, but otherwise she was unmarked. Hannah gathered her into her arms and wept bitterly. Then she fetched bowls and cloths and washed and tended her most tenderly. When all was decently arranged, she sat by the bed and talked to the dead girl. The daylight died away and night came. Still she sat murmuring words of love to her dead child.

When the room grew grey with the dawn light, she got up and went to her own room. There she made simple preparations for a journey. She left all neat and tidy, then, cloaked and bonneted, returned to Catlin's room. She bent over the bed and once more smoothed back the hair, now dried to its usual soft ash brown, from the girl's cold face. She whispered a few last words then went out of the room leaving the door open behind her. As she did so, she thought, 'the funeral, I shall not be there!' Then, 'let them deal with that. I have done here now. I have said my farewells...'

She walked up the winding drive to the road above. The storm had died away and the air was completely still and silent except for the icy trickling of flood water in the ditches below the hedges. She walked to where the wider road joined the lane. She paused there and rested as she looked back at Ty

Garreg. Then, straightening her back and grasping her small bag firmly, she took the road to the right. The click of her boot heels echoed across the hills as she strode quickly and without a backward glance away from her old life and into the new.

1		25		49		73	
2		26		50		74	
3		27		51		75	
4		28		52		76	
5		29		53		77	
6		30		54		78	
7		31		55		79	
8 ~~JUL 2007~~				56		80	
9		33		57		81	
10		34		58		82	
11		35		59		83	
12		36		60		84	12/99
13		37		61		85	
14		38		62		86	
15		39 5/05		63		87	
16		40		64		88	
17		41		65		89	
18		42		66		90	
19		43		67		91	
20		44		68		92	
21		45		69		COMMUNITY SERVICES	
22		46		70			
23		47		71		NPT/111	
24		48		72			